To Whom It Never Reached

To Whom
It Never Reached

Bhavya Barai

NU VOICE
PRESS

First published by NU VOICE PRESS 2025
An imprint of Hubhawks Pvt. Ltd
www.nuvoicepress.com

This is a work of fiction. Space and time have been rearranged to suit the convenience of the book. Except for public figures, hotels, and institution names, any resemblance to persons living or dead or the real events are purely coincidental. The opinions expressed in the book are those of the characters, and should not be confused with that of the Author.

ISBN: 978-81-993013-8-2
Typeset by Pooja Sharma
Printed at Manipal Technologies Limited, Manipal
Published by Nu Voice Press

To the unheard, the unseen, and the unread—

To those who wrote but never sent,

Who felt but never spoke,

Who lived with silence heavy on their hearts.

This is for you.

And to the ones who taught me that words, even if unsent, still hold the power to heal.

We live in a world overflowing with noise, yet so many words remain unsaid.

This story was never meant to be told in loud

declarations or perfect conclusions.

It was born from the unfinished—from the *scribbled*

letters that never left the drawer,

the *truths we tell ourselves in the quiet of night*,

the *memories tucked beneath decades of silence.*

To Whom It Never Reached began as a simple question:

What happens to the words we never say?

In chasing that answer, I found a boy haunted not by ghosts, but by **silences**.

A grandfather who spoke through letters.

A father who forgot how to feel.

And a legacy built not of achievements, but of

emotional inheritance.

This isn't a tale of grand victories.

It's about the *fragile, deeply human attempts at connection*—

about **grief**, *guilt*, **art**, *memory*, and above all, **healing**.

I wrote this not to give you answers,

but to help you *sit with your own questions a little longer.*

If you've ever *loved silently, mourned deeply,*

or *held back a truth until it ached*—

this book is for you.

What's Inside

ACT I: Discovery & Decision

"The past never dies.
It just hides in boxes we're too afraid to open."

Chapter 1: The Funeral

The sky had the decency to be grey.

Ruhan stood among a sea of familiar strangers, their faces dulled by grief, smoke, and time. The sandalwood fire crackled behind him, coughing ash into the breeze. Somewhere within that pyre lay the man who once taught him how to hold a brush like a whisper.

He didn't shed a tear. *Not when the call came. Not during the long train ride back home. Not now.*

The priest's voice droned in Sanskrit—ancient syllables clashing with modern discomfort. A few relatives muttered their responses, while others discreetly checked their phones, as if grief could be postponed until the notifications stopped pinging.

The smoke clung to Ruhan's clothes, weaving through flames as they curled around the wood. *He hated fire. It always consumed more than it gave.*

"He would have wanted you to speak," someone whispered beside him.

He nodded but said nothing. What could he possibly say about a man who spoke more through silence than sermons? *His grandfather wasn't the kind you eulogize.* ***He was the kind you remember in echoes—***

a pipe's scent on an old coat,

a sketchbook with pages left blank,

a mug stained with tea and time.

He clenched his hands behind his back, fingers tracing the groove of his thumb, like a silent metronome. There had been words he might've said once. But they had scattered long ago—with the move, with the distance, with time.

Across the clearing, his father stood with arms crossed. Still tall. Still unreadable.

Their eyes met—once.

Acknowledgment, not greeting.

Grief hadn't softened the air between them. It only made the silence heavier.

They hadn't spoken properly in three years. That silence, too, had become something inherited.

After the rituals, as the crowd thinned, Ruhan wandered into the ancestral house—half museum, half mausoleum. Every corner held dust and memory in equal measure. The walls, once ivory, were now the colour of old bones. *The air was thick with mothballs, incense, and oil paint—a scent he hadn't realized he'd missed.*

It was quieter inside than he expected. Not empty, just... still. *Like time itself had agreed to pause out of respect.*

He passed the wooden swing in the hallway, now tilted at an odd angle, one of its chains rusted. The floor creaked beneath his steps. Portraits lined the walls, none of them smiling. Everything looked like it had settled into its place long ago—and stayed untouched, unlaughed at, unloved since.

In the living room, his father was removing the garland from a black-and-white portrait. He set it aside gently, then began folding a shawl, clearing space with the measured movements of someone avoiding conversation.

Ruhan lingered at the doorway, uncertain.

"You'll take the studio, right?"

His father's voice didn't carry expectation. It carried a conclusion.

"It still has your things."

"Yeah" Ruhan said.

There was a pause—the kind that might've been filled by a question, once.

But neither man stepped toward it.

Upstairs, the studio waited like a closed throat.

Dust swirled in shafts of fading light through the wooden blinds. The easel still stood in the corner—a ghost of an unfinished canvas clinging to it, colours dried mid-thought. On the desk: a scattering of brushes, a chipped ceramic palette, a small brass box with peeling lacquer.

He stepped in. The air smelled of turpentine and memory.

For a moment, he didn't move. Just stood in the doorway, like he was afraid his presence would disturb something sacred. Or wake something sleeping.

Then he walked to the centre of the room and sat on the old stool.

The cushion let out a soft sigh beneath his weight.

The silence here wasn't heavy.

It was holy.

Like the walls were holding their breath.

He ran a hand along the edge of the table.

Faint streaks of blue and ochre still stained the wood—remnants of older afternoons.

And suddenly, without warning, a memory surfaced.

He was ten.

Sitting on the floor, legs crossed, trying to copy the way his grandfather held a brush.

"Like this?" he had asked, lifting his tiny hand.

His grandfather had smiled—not with his mouth, but with his eyes—and adjusted Ruhan's grip.

"Not like you're holding a sword," he had said, "like you're holding a secret."

Ruhan had laughed back then, unaware of what it truly meant. Now, he did.

The weight of that moment sat beside him, as real as dust.

He looked around the room.

Something was missing.

And something...was waiting.

He rose, slowly, and approached the brass box.

It was heavier than he remembered. The lid bore tiny scratches, faded fingerprints. Paint flecks clung to the edges like tiny constellations.

He didn't open it.

Not yet.

He traced the top with one finger, then turned it gently—and there, on the underside, faint and worn but unmistakable, was his name.

"Ruhan"

Etched in his grandfather's handwriting.

Not carved with a tool. Not meant to last.

Just...left.

Like a whisper, he had meant to hear when it was time.

Ruhan sat down again and placed the box in his lap. He didn't move for a while. Outside, a bird called once, before the silence returned.

His eyes rested on the mark—that single word—as if it were a door.

He blinked and felt the first tear slip down, quiet as the morning light.

Not grief. Not yet.

But the opening of something long buried.

A soft click, inside his chest.

As if something had just...begun.

Chapter 2: The Box in the Attic

The hinges creaked—soft, reluctant—as if the box itself had forgotten how to open.

Ruhan lifted the lid slowly, expecting nothing. Or everything. **He wasn't sure which would hurt more.**

Inside, wrapped in a faded red cloth, was a bundle of letters—bound with thin, brittle twine that looked like it might turn to dust with a breath.

They didn't look like artifacts.

They looked like they had waited.

He hesitated.

There was something sacred about them—not religious, but intentional. *As if they weren't meant to be hidden, just... postponed.*

He untied the string.

It snapped without resistance.

The cloth fell open like a wound.

Dozens of letters. All handwritten. All carefully folded. None addressed to him—at least not on top.

He picked the first.

"To Arvind"

No envelope. No date. *Just that name, and his grandfather's quiet, graceful handwriting—the kind that curved as if it had learned to speak through silence.*

Ruhan opened it carefully, fingers tracing the edge like it might bleed.

"I have carried this silence longer than I should have."

That single line sat heavy on the page. The rest unfolded slowly—a memory, a mistake, a friendship abandoned in the shadow of pride. There was a mention of a railway platform. Of a quarrel that should've ended with an embrace, not absence.

It wasn't self-pitying—just honest, with regret lacing every sentence, subdued rather than theatrical.

When he reached the end, Ruhan realized he hadn't taken a breath in nearly a minute.

He set the letter down.

The silence in the room had changed. It wasn't sacred anymore.

It was charged. Watchful.

He looked at the box again.

A hundred more silences lay inside.

Some addressed in Gujarati, one in flowing Urdu, a few in halting English, and near the bottom, were few letters, unmistakable in their weights, addressed:

"To My Son"

He didn't touch them.

His fingers hovered, then withdrew—as if the papers could burn. *He wasn't ready. Not for those ones. Maybe not for any of them.*

He leaned back, closing his eyes for just a second.

And that's when it came—*a memory, soft as a brushstroke.*

A younger version of him, seated cross-legged on the floor of this very studio.

His grandfather, above him, was painting without looking at the canvas.

Music playing faintly—old ghazals drifting in from the hallway.

"Not everything worth feeling is worth framing," his grandfather had said, pausing mid-stroke.

Back then, Ruhan thought he was talking about art.

Now, it felt like something else entirely.

He stood and reached for another letter.

"To Devraj"

The name jolted something.

A childhood guest? A name once whispered during arguments downstairs? He couldn't place it.

This one read more like a poem than a letter.

"You were the war I chose to lose, and the brother I never dared to win back."

Page after page—a story of jealousy, ego, and the ache of losing someone still alive. His grandfather's words trembled between confession and surrender.

Ruhan folded the letter and set it gently beside the first one.

He didn't feel like a reader.

He felt like a trespasser.

These weren't just words.

They were unfinished conversations—and somehow, they had chosen him to finish them.

As he shifted the stack, a smaller envelope slid free—pale blue, with a faint marigold imprint on one corner.

There was no name on the outside, only a wax seal, long since cracked.

Inside it was a preserved marigold, brittle and sun-faded.

The letter was softer. More prose than apology.

"We were just children sharing silence in an adult world.

You taught me how to cut mangoes without touching the seed.

How to hide tears during lightning storms.

And I...

I left before you could teach me how to stay."

Signed:

—Radhika

His grandfather's sister.

Ruhan had heard her name only once—in a hushed tone, during a tense dinner. *A falling out. Something about inheritance. Or ideology. Or both.*

This wasn't a letter written to her.

It was one from her.

And his grandfather had kept it.

Ruhan folded the letter gently and returned the marigold to its place. *He placed it beside the others as if it belonged there.*

A knock on the door startled him.

Too sharp. Too sudden.

His breath caught.

"Lunch," his father said from the other side.

"You'll eat?"

Ruhan hesitated. "Yeah. I'll be down."

The knob turned halfway—then stopped.

Silence.

He sat for a while, motionless. *The moment had cracked, but not broken.*

He looked back at the box.

There were stories in there—pieces of a man he thought he knew, now unravelling in cursive.

And somewhere beneath them all,

one letter waited for him.

That's when he noticed it—something peeking from beneath the paint-stiff cloth in the box's corner.

A sketch.

Drawn in charcoal. Edges curled. The paper warped with time.

He lifted it carefully.

It was a portrait.

Of him.

Maybe sixteen years old. Sad-eyed. Unposed. Almost unfinished.

It didn't look like a study.

It looked like a memory.

He turned it over.

"*Forgive the likeness. He wouldn't sit still.*"

His grandfather's handwriting.

But Ruhan didn't remember sitting for it.

And yet...the shading. The slight tilt of his head. The flicker in the eyes—it was too real, too precise, to be imagined.

Had his grandfather drawn it from memory?

Or from feeling?

He placed the sketch beside the marigold-stained letter.

But something gnawed at him. Not the words. Not the face.

It was what they didn't say.

How much had been left out?

How much had he missed just by not asking, by growing up too fast, too far away?

He looked into the box again.

A letter near the bottom was marked in red ink—thicker, almost angry.

But he didn't touch it. Not yet.

Instead, he stood.

He left the sketch and the marigold letter on the desk, side by side, like offerings.

And this time, when he turned to leave,

he didn't close the box.

Something inside it was still breathing.

And maybe, after all this time,

it was finally ready to speak.

Chapter 3: Ghosts in the Studio

The morning light bled through the shutters like it didn't want to be there.

Ruhan lay on the mattress, eyes open but unfocused. The ceiling fan hummed above him, slow and rhythmic, but somehow too loud. *It was the kind of sleep that doesn't rest you—just divides the night from the next set of hours. In his mind, the box was still open, the letters still breathing.*

He hadn't dreamt of anything in particular. But he woke with the weight of a conversation he hadn't had.

The sketch still lay on the studio desk, the charcoal lines catching just enough light to make it seem like the face could blink. He'd thought, in the moment, that it was nothing more than a sketch. *But now, in daylight, it felt different. Like the sketch wasn't something his grandfather had made of him, but for him.*

Or worse, instead of him.

He sat up, bones slow to cooperate, and moved toward the desk. *The marigold from Radhika's letter had wilted more in the night, the edges curling inward like it was listening to something.*

The box was still open.

Ruhan didn't reach for another letter yet. He just stood there, letting the stillness thicken. The air had changed—he was sure of it. *It wasn't a scent or a temperature. It was...presence.*

Something was waiting. Or maybe watching.

He picked up his sketchbook—old, worn, its corners dog-eared from years of disuse. The first few pages were blank, too clean. Then: scattered hands, awkward profiles, fragments of faces never finished. An eye. A lip. A bruise, maybe.

He found one sketch that had bothered him back in college. A faceless figure seated in a chair, head bowed, hands loose like a string at the ends of its arms. He remembered drawing it during a late-night breakdown he never told anyone about. His professor said it "lacked form." His friend said it was "weirdly sad."

His grandfather had never seen it.

Maybe that was a good thing.

He turned to a blank page. Picked up a pencil and tried to draw a line.

Nothing.

The lead hovered, unsure. His fingers curled, then relaxed.

Still nothing.

"Stop performing," he whispered to himself. "It's just you."

But the pencil didn't move.

Somewhere inside him, a pressure had been building. *Not panic, not really—just a tightening, like an emotion trying to form before language could catch it.*

He stood and walked to the canvas on the easel—the old one his grandfather had left unfinished. Layers of paint, dusty and cracked now, stared back at him like a half-forgotten memory that refused to fade.

Ruhan reached out and touched it. The texture was brittle, like skin stretched too long in the sun. And yet—beneath the dust, there was life. A story in colour he couldn't yet read.

Something shifted on the desk.

Just a brush falling over.

Or maybe not.

He turned quickly. Nothing had changed.

Still, his eyes moved toward the box.

Still open.

Still full.

And near the front now—pushed slightly forward as if it wanted to be seen—was a letter with no name. Just initials:

"R.M."

He frowned. That wasn't a name he recognized.

He hesitated. Then reached for it.

The paper was thinner than the others, almost translucent.

He unfolded it.

"You said a promise was just a story waiting to betray itself.

You were right, R.M. But you also promised to stay.

So where did you go?"

"I didn't mean to become the man you left.

But I did."

"And I have lived in that sentence longer than any home."

It ended abruptly. No sign-off. Just a date at the bottom: 1987.

Ruhan stared at it for a long time.

There was something sharp in those lines. Not just regret—guilt sharpened into clarity.

This wasn't a goodbye.

It was a confession.

He folded the letter again and placed it carefully beside the others.

He had questions now.

Not about the people in the letters—

But about the man who wrote them.

Outside, the wind had picked up.

It scraped against the shutters like fingers testing for cracks. Leaves danced across the terrace. Somewhere below, a bicycle bell rang twice—the same way it used to when the chaiwala passed by in the late afternoons.

The studio, however, remained still.

Ruhan pulled open the narrow drawer in the desk. Inside: a few half-used pastels, an old fountain pen dried beyond rescue, and a yellowing envelope addressed in Gujarati.

He didn't open it. Not yet.

His mind was still circling the R.M. letter. The initials stirred nothing familiar, but the tone—sharp, direct, wounded—echoed like a note struck deep inside a hollow instrument. He kept hearing that line:

"I didn't mean to become the man you left."

It didn't sound like his grandfather at all. And yet, it couldn't have come from anyone else.

How many versions of this man had existed?

How many people had met a different version of him—and carried it like a myth that never matched the man Ruhan knew?

He moved to the window and cracked it open slightly. The scent of the outside world—wet earth, frying oil, and drying paint—slipped in.

The city was still going about its day. His grief didn't slow the market down, didn't delay the bus routes, didn't make the school kids quiet down in the lane outside.

Life, indifferent and unbothered.

Ruhan returned to the canvas.

A single stroke. That's all he wanted to attempt.

He dipped a brush—one of his grandfather's—and loaded it with watered-down sienna. The bristles held the pigment like breath.

The moment his brush touched the canvas, he froze.

It felt wrong. Not bad. Just...wrong.

As if the canvas didn't belong to him.

He let out a breath and pulled back.

And that's when he noticed it—

On the wall, high above the shelf where an old teapot sat collecting dust, something shimmered faintly in the slanted light.

A sketch.

Pinned beneath a paperweight.

He hadn't seen it the night before.

Ruhan climbed onto the stool to reach it. The paper was coarse and thick. Another portrait. But not of him.

This one was of a woman—half-smiling, eyes caught in motion, like she was about to turn away or speak. Her hair was tied in a long braid—a small bindi at her forehead.

But it wasn't the face that struck him.

It was the caption beneath it:

"She said I saw her better than she ever saw herself.

That's how I knew I had to let her go."

No signature.

No name.

No date.

Ruhan sat back down, sketch and brush both forgotten.

The ghosts in this studio weren't the floating, wailing kind.

They were observing.

They were patient.

They waited inside lines, behind ink, inside every "what if" that had never made it into a letter.

His phone buzzed from somewhere in the next room. He ignored it.

His fingers itched now—not to paint, but to draw. To record what he was feeling before it vanished.

He grabbed his own sketchbook and turned to a blank page.

Charcoal this time.

A face—not a specific one, just fragments.

Tired eyes. A mouth mid-sentence. Shoulders slightly slumped. Hands not clenched, but not open either.

He kept sketching.

Page after page.

Faces began to form. Not from memory—but from echo.

Was this what his grandfather had meant? Is everything worth feeling also worth framing?

Or was this exactly what needed to be framed?

Unspoken emotion. Unfinished conversations.

Maybe art was just the letter you wrote to someone who could never read it.

When he finally looked up, it was almost evening.

The light had gone gold and soft, slanting across the floor like a gentle goodbye.

He stood.

Returned to the box.

Picked a new letter.

This one had a seal. Black wax.

He cracked it open and found, inside, a single sentence:

"I never told you because I knew you'd stay—and that would've ruined you."

There was no context.

No name.

No date.

Just that.

And folded inside it, a ticket stub—worn, folded, with the name of a city he'd never been to.

A whisper of a story, half-burnt.

He placed it back in the box.

He would need to follow some of these.

Maybe not all. But some.

Because someone out there had waited.

Just like these letters.

That night, the rain arrived quietly.

It tapped the windows like someone too polite to demand entry. Outside, the world dissolved into shadows and water. Inside the studio, Ruhan sat with a cup of coffee, the box open on the desk beside him in the candlelight. He hadn't touched it in hours.

He sat with his knees to his chest on the floor, sketchbook beside him, listening to the soft symphony of storm and silence. He'd lit an incense stick out of habit. *The smoke curled through the room like a second presence—graceful, intrusive, uninvited.*

His latest drawing sat half-done. Not a person this time, but the box itself.

Open. Glowing.

Except he hadn't drawn what was inside.

"Just lines. Empty space. Waiting."

His eyes drifted to the letter with the initials R.M. again. Still folded, still too loud for silence. And then to the sketch of the woman. The unnamed one with the soft braid and eyes like parting words.

So many unfinished things.

Maybe that's what this room was built on.

Not art.

Not legacy.

But the weight of what people couldn't say.

He flipped to a blank page.

Wrote two words in the centre.

"Who else?"

There were names in those letters he'd never heard before.

Places he'd never been.

A whole map of his grandfather's life—folded and hidden like contraband inside a brass box.

And now it was in his hands.

Ruhan ran his fingers through his hair. **He could feel a new kind of restlessness crawling under his skin.** A tightness behind his ribs, like he hadn't fully exhaled since reading the first letter.

He wanted to know more.

But more meant risk.

More meant—he might not like the man he found at the end of these pages.

He reached toward the box again, almost without thinking.

And paused.

Because something had shifted.

One of the letters—one he hadn't seen before—was now near the front. Slightly tilted, as if it had been lifted and dropped again.

Ruhan stared at it.

There was no wind. No fan. No open windows.

And yet...

The letter had moved.

He leaned in.

"To Whom It Never Reached."

His breath caught in his throat.

It wasn't addressed to anyone.

Or maybe—

It was addressed to everyone.

Or him.

He didn't open it.

Not yet.

Instead, he gently placed it back, deeper in the stack.

Whatever that letter held, it didn't want to be rushed.

Some truths needed to ferment.

Some ghosts needed to knock twice.

He cleaned up the space, one thing at a time. Brushed charcoal dust from the desk. Re-capped the ink. Folded the sketches, placing them in a folder that hadn't seen new pages in years.

And finally, as the candle burned low, he walked to the window.

The rain was letting up. Just a drizzle now.

And in the hazy reflection of the glass, he caught something unexpected.

Not a shape.

Not a shadow.

A colour.

On the canvas behind him—the one his grandfather had left unfinished—there was a new streak of ochre across the lower right corner.

He hadn't touched the paints since morning.

He turned quickly.

Nothing moved.

The brush still sat dry. The palette untouched.

The ochre was there, like it had always been.

Like he'd missed it.

Or like...something hadn't.

He didn't sleep that night. Not deeply, anyway.

Just drifted in and out of memories that weren't his.

He dreamed of old hands sketching by candlelight.

Of a woman with a braid who kept walking away.

Of a letter trying to speak through flame and fog.

When morning came, he didn't feel rested.

But he felt...ready.

Tomorrow, maybe, he would deliver one of the letters.

Or write one of his own.

But the thought of it lingered, unsettling, like the pause before a confession.

Because what would he even write?

Who would it be to?

He didn't have the answers.

Only the weight of questions passed down like heirlooms, *folded between pages, and silence.*

As he turned to leave the studio, something stopped him.

On the desk, just beside the sketchbook, the topmost letter had shifted again. Slightly. Just enough to make him notice.

He hadn't touched it.

He stared at it for a long moment.

Then reached forward and closed the lid of the box.

Not yet, he told himself.

But soon.

And as he left the room, the light behind him dimmed, leaving the studio—and the stories waiting inside it—quiet once more.

Chapter 4: First Letter, First Step

The sun spilled into the studio in slices, filtering through wooden slats and drifting specks of dust in the curtains. Ruhan stirred awake on the daybed by the wall, blanket half-tangled at his ankles, sketchbook pressed open across his chest like a second heart.

He hadn't truly slept. His body had gone still, yes—but his mind had paced in circles all night, dragging memory and doubt behind it.

Now, the light felt different. Less forgiving. More expectant.

He sat up slowly.

The brass box still sat on the desk, lid closed, but not locked. It didn't need to be. *The letters inside didn't escape—they waited. Patient, like breath held too long.*

Ruhan stood, stretched, and crossed the room barefoot.

He didn't reach for the box right away.

Instead, he touched the canvas again. *Still unfinished. Still silent. But maybe, just maybe, it didn't feel so foreign now.*

A breath. Then another.

He turned back to the desk and opened the lid.

The letters greeted him like old voices in a hallway.

He didn't touch the ones addressed "To My Son". Not yet.

Instead, he found it easily—To Arvind.

The first one he had read. The quiet one. The wound stitched in regret.

He ran a thumb over the edge, then folded it and placed it into a blank envelope. He didn't seal it. It didn't feel like it should be sealed.

As if it might still need air.

The dining table was already set when he came downstairs. His father sat at the far end, hunched slightly, eyes on the newspaper but not really reading. A bowl of lukewarm poha and a cup of tea sat untouched in front of him.

Ruhan sat across from him in silence.

The clink of the spoon against his steel plate felt too loud. He didn't know what to say, and his father didn't look like he was expecting anything.

It was the kind of breakfast that had always existed between them: functional, flavourless, fragile.

Until—

"You're going out?" his father asked suddenly, not looking up.

Ruhan blinked. "Yeah. Just into town."

A pause. Not disapproval. Just air.

"You remember the way?"

The question startled him.

"I think so," Ruhan said. "I mean...I'll figure it out."

His father nodded once and returned to his paper.

A sentence had been exchanged. That was new.

By late morning, Ruhan stood outside the old train station.

The air smelled like rust, fried snacks, and countless footsteps layered over decades. There was a tea stall tucked into the far corner, shaded by a peeling green tarp—the one mentioned in the letter. It had to be.

He waited in line behind two older men debating loudly about politics and cricket, and then ordered a cutting chai.

"Do you know someone named Arvind?" he asked, cautiously, while the chaiwala poured tea into cups with practiced ease.

The man squinted. "Arvindbhai? The painter?"

Ruhan's heart caught in his chest.

"I—yes. He was friends with my grandfather. Harish."

The chaiwala tilted his head slightly, then grunted. "Bungalowwala artist Harish?"

"Yeah."

The man nodded. "They used to come here. Long time ago. Arvind comes sometimes still. Lives just two streets down, near the tailor's gully. Ask for Mehta House."

Ruhan smiled in thanks, surprised at how easily the thread had tugged free.

"Tell him Mitesh from Railway Chai sent you," the man added, almost offhand, handing him the cup.

The tea was scalding. And exactly right.

Fifteen minutes later, Ruhan stood before a pale blue building with sun-bleached shutters. Mehta House was written in faded paint above the entrance, like it hadn't been touched up since the nineties.

There were plants on the balcony. And wind chimes that moved without sound.

He climbed the narrow staircase, the letter tucked inside his notebook like a secret.

At the second-floor landing, he paused. The door in front of him was ajar. Inside, he could hear a radio playing an old Lata Mangeshkar song softly—*Lag Jaa Gale, one of his grandfather's favourites.*

He knocked gently.

Nothing.

Then again, slightly firmer.

A moment later, the door creaked open, and an old man with sharp cheekbones and a weathered cotton kurta stood there, blinking at him.

His eyes were tired, but alert. They narrowed slightly as they scanned Ruhan's face.

"Yes?"

Ruhan stepped forward. "Are you...Arvindbhai?"

The man didn't answer right away.

Then, slowly, his expression shifted—not into recognition, but into memory.

"You're Harish's boy."

It wasn't a question.

Ruhan nodded, unsure why his throat suddenly felt dry.

"I have something for you."

He held out the envelope.

Arvind didn't take it.

Not immediately.

He just looked at it.

Then at Ruhan.

Then back to the letter.

"You'd better come in," he said quietly. ***"That letter... has waited too long."***

The apartment was small but full of light. Afternoon sun spilled through gauze curtains, warming the tiled floor and bouncing off the glass of old photo frames. A few canvases leaned against the far wall—unfinished, *like conversations paused mid-sentence.*

Arvind walked with slow care, his spine bent not only by age, but something heavier. Time. Memory. Maybe both.

He motioned toward a wooden chair, its cushions worn thin.

"Sit, sit. I'll get my glasses."

Ruhan nodded silently, settling into the chair. He kept the envelope in his lap like it might disappear if he let go.

The room smelled like camphor and turpentine—the scent of places that have known both illness and art.

Arvind returned and sat across from him, adjusting his wire-rimmed spectacles. Then, wordlessly, he extended his hand.

Ruhan offered the letter.

The old man held it as if it were something delicate—*not fragile, but sacred.* His eyes scanned the handwriting, and his breath caught, just slightly.

"Still the same hand," he murmured.

He didn't ask how Ruhan found it. Or why he brought it. He simply unfolded the letter and began to read.

Ruhan tried not to stare, but every flicker in Arvind's eyes pulled at him. The way his lips pressed into a line. The way he paused once—just once—to close his eyes.

It took only minutes to read.

But the silence after felt eternal.

Finally, Arvind set the letter on the table between them.

"He wrote this?" he asked, though he already knew.

Ruhan nodded.

"Never sent it," he said quietly. "I found it after he died."

Arvind leaned back, arms crossed over his chest. He was quiet for so long, Ruhan thought he might not say anything at all.

Then—

"He always said too little," Arvind said. "Even when we were young. But when he did speak...it stayed."

Ruhan waited.

Arvind's gaze turned toward the window, toward something far beyond it.

"We were like mirror edges, Harish and I. *Too alike to bend, too proud to heal.* We built dreams together. Painted side by side. Spoke of revolutions over tea and shared sketchbooks. And then..."

He trailed off.

"Then something small broke. And *we let it grow.*"

Ruhan leaned forward slightly. "The letter said it was...a fight? At the station?"

Arvind gave a soft, bitter laugh.

"A ridiculous one. About a gallery showing. He thought I'd betrayed him. I thought he'd abandoned me. Maybe we were both right. Or both wrong."

He shook his head.

"He left. Didn't speak to me again. I sent letters. He never replied. I thought..."

He tapped the paper.

"I thought he didn't care anymore."

Ruhan felt the air grow heavier. The ache in Arvind's voice wasn't just from the past. It was from the realization that the past had never truly left.

"He carried it," Ruhan said. "All these years."

Arvind looked at him—really looked.

"And you? Why bring it?"

Ruhan hesitated.

He didn't have an answer that could be put into words.

"Because I didn't know him," he said finally. "Not really. But I want to. And this...it felt like something I wasn't meant to keep to myself."

Arvind nodded slowly. His fingers traced the edge of the letter once more.

"Then maybe this letter came to the right person."

They sat in silence again, but this time it didn't feel heavy. It felt held—like something sacred passing between generations.

After a while, Arvind stood and walked to a small wooden drawer. He pulled something from it—a folded photograph, yellowed at the edges.

He returned and handed it to Ruhan.

It was an old black-and-white photo—Harish and Arvind, both in their twenties. Paint-smudged, smiling, sitting on a train platform with cups of tea in their hands.

Ruhan stared at it as if it were proof that stories could be real.

"*We were fools*," Arvind said. "*But beautiful ones*."

Ruhan smiled, gently folding the photo.

"Thank you," he said.

Arvind shook his head. "No, thank you. For giving me the ending I didn't know I needed."

Outside, the sun had slipped westward. The air felt different. A little lighter. A little clearer.

As Ruhan walked back toward the station, *the weight in his chest had shifted. Not gone, but moved.*

He sat on the train with the photo in his pocket and the sketchbook in his lap.

For the first time in months, he drew—not from imagination, but from memory. Arvind's lined face, softened by forgiveness. His grandfather's younger eyes, half-smiling from the past. And between them, the letter.

He didn't sketch them apart.

He sketched them together—finally, in the same frame.

The house was quiet when Ruhan returned.

Not just still—quiet in the way a place gets when something inside it has changed. He walked in with soft steps, not to disturb the air.

His father wasn't in the living room. The television was off. No half-read paper lay on the table. The only sound was the ticking of the wall clock and the faint buzz of a ceiling fan that had long outlived its grace.

Ruhan climbed the stairs slowly.

The studio welcomed him like a place not quite empty. Like it had been waiting. The smell of paint, paper, and the faintest scent of rain still lingered in the corners.

He dropped his sketchbook on the desk and sat.

He didn't open the box. He didn't need to—not yet.

Instead, he reached for his pencil, turned to a fresh page, and began to draw again.

Not because he was ready.

But because something had shifted.

He sketched the shape of Arvind's shoulders. The gentle slouch, the way age curled him in but never folded him entirely.

Then he added his grandfather—not as an old man, but as the young version from the photograph. Smiling. Open. Before pride and distance complicated everything.

He shaded them with care, letting the lines speak the things neither of them had said aloud.

When he finished, the light outside had turned amber—that golden moment between day and dusk.

He sat back, stared at the sketch, and let himself feel...not pride, not peace, but presence.

For the first time in a long while, Ruhan felt like he wasn't just passing through his own life. He was in it.

Later, as the sky deepened into blue and the crickets began their soft orchestra, there was a knock at the studio door.

His father.

He didn't come in. Just stood in the hallway, a silhouette against the corridor light.

"I...saw your bag downstairs," he said. "You went somewhere?"

Ruhan looked up. "Yeah. Delivered a letter."

His father shifted slightly, unsure of what to say next.

"Someone important?" he finally asked.

Ruhan thought for a moment. "To him? Yes. An old friend. *They hadn't spoken in decades.*"

There was a silence that wasn't tense—just uncertain.

Then, to Ruhan's surprise, his father took a small step forward.

"He...left one for me too, didn't he?"

It wasn't a question. Not really.

Ruhan met his eyes for the first time in what felt like years.

"Yes, more than one," he said quietly. "But I haven't read them. "And I haven't even touched them yet."

His father gave a small nod.

"Good."

Then, after a pause, he added—

"When you're ready to give them...I'll be here."

And just like that, he turned and walked away.

Not cold.

Not warm.

Just open. For the first time.

That night, Ruhan didn't open another letter.

He sat by the window with the sketchbook in his lap and the studio washed in moonlight. Outside, the city murmured—cars in the distance, a stray dog barking somewhere near the gate, the hum of life continuing.

Inside, the box sat closed on the desk. Not hidden. Not sealed. Just... resting.

He traced the edges of his drawing with his fingers.

Then, without thinking too hard about it, he flipped to a new page.

And began to write.

Not a sketch. Not a letter.

But something in between.

He didn't know who it was for.

But it felt like a reply.

To all the silences. To all the things that never reached anyone.

The next morning, the light had a different kind of warmth—gentler, somehow, as if it no longer tried to chase shadows away but invited them to stay awhile.

Ruhan brewed his own tea. His hands moved without urgency, his breath steady. Something had loosened inside him—not resolved, not explained, but no longer clenched.

At the table, his father was already seated, peeling an orange with clinical precision. He looked up briefly. Their eyes met. No words exchanged, just a faint nod.

That was enough.

Back in the studio, Ruhan opened the box again.

This time, there was no hesitation.

He didn't pick the heaviest letter or the most fragile-looking one. He didn't search for meaning. He just reached in, letting his fingers stop where they would.

It was simply addressed as:

"To Ravi—I remember the war, but not the peace."

He sat with it for a while before opening it.

The handwriting was shakier in this one. Older. Less polished. There were misspellings. Crossed-out words. A rawness that wasn't in the others.

The first few lines were strange—almost cryptic. Mentions of 1965. Of heat and blood. *Of cigarettes smoked behind barricades. And a photo that never arrived home.*

Ruhan paused midway through the letter.

He had no idea who Ravi was. But this letter felt different. Urgent. It hummed in his hand as if it wanted to be heard aloud, not just read.

He turned to his notebook and scribbled the words that stood out:

"He said war makes poets of cowards and cowards of heroes."

A chill ran through him. He didn't know why.

But the letter had weight. *Not only in words—but also in history*. And something told him **this one might be harder to deliver.**

He gently folded it back, placed it at the top of the box, and stared at it for a long time.

That evening, as the sun dipped below the edge of the rooftops, Ruhan sat on the studio floor, surrounded by fragments of lives he didn't yet understand—people he'd never met, feelings that had been buried longer than he'd been alive.

And yet, somehow, they felt like his to carry.

Not as a burden, but as a bridge.

He looked around the room—at the canvas, the brushes, the box.

And, **he whispered to no one in particular:**

"I think I'm starting to hear you."

ACT II: The Journey

"We don't just inherit names or blood—
we inherit silence, too.
And to break it is to begin becoming."

Chapter 5: The War Brother

The letter had no return address, only a name:

"To Ravi—I remember the war, but not the peace."

Ruhan had read it three times in silence before something in it—maybe a date, or a battalion number—led him down a path of phone calls and tea-stained directories. A retired army officer in an outer district. A village that hadn't changed much since the ceasefire. A name that the locals still spoke with respect, yet always in a hush, as if burdened by more than they could put into words.

Himmat Singh.

The gate to his house now rusted, but was once painted with care. A small patch of marigolds bloomed on either side. The house itself was plain—whitewashed, square, low-roofed—but the porch held an air of discipline, like every object had been assigned its place and had damn well better stay there.

Ruhan knocked twice.

Silence.

Then the creak of a wooden chair shifting, and the shuffle of slow feet.

The door opened.

And there he stood—taller than Ruhan expected, though his back was curved and his eyes deeply set in the hollow of age. He wore a white kurta, frayed at the collar, and over it...a coat.

Faded olive green. Shoulder epaulettes dulled to brass buttons polished by time.

"You're not from the post office," the man said flatly.

Ruhan gave a nervous smile. "No, sir. I'm not."

"Then you've either come to sell me something I don't need...or you've brought something I forgot."

Ruhan held out the letter, folded in its original shape.

"It's about Ravi."

The old man didn't reach for it. He just looked at Ruhan, expression unreadable.

"You a reporter?"

"No."

"Historian?"

"No."

"Then why carry dead men's words?"

That made Ruhan pause.

"Because they're not dead," he said quietly. *"Not if they're still waiting to be heard."*

Something softened in Himmat's face. Just slightly. Like a door not yet open, but no longer locked.

He stepped aside.

"Tea first. Then ghosts."

The house was clean. Sparse. The living room held only a cot, a small shelf of books, and a cabinet full of medals that didn't gleam the way you'd expect. They looked like they'd rather be forgotten.

The tea came strong, unsweetened, and served in metal cups. The kind that stayed warm forever.

They sat across from each other—Himmat on the cot, Ruhan on a wooden stool.

Ruhan placed the letter on the table between them.

The old man didn't touch it right away. He simply stared at it.

"He wrote it?"

"Yes," Ruhan said. "My grandfather."

Himmat's brow furrowed. "Name?"

"Harish."

Silence.

A muscle twitched in Himmat's jaw.

"Harish Desai?"

Ruhan nodded.

"He was with me in '65. Border camp. *'Paintbrushes and prayers.'* He said bullets made him nervous."

Ruhan smiled faintly. "He was a painter."

"He was a coward," Himmat said, not unkindly. "But he stayed. Even when he shouldn't have."

He reached for the letter. Opened it.

Read.

It didn't take long. It wasn't a long letter.

But it wasn't short either.

Some words take longer to travel, even when they're already on paper.

When he finished, Himmat didn't speak for a long time.

Instead, he reached behind the cot and pulled out a small wooden box. The hinges squeaked like they hadn't moved in years.

Inside, among old service documents and photographs, was a medal.

And a photograph. Two men. Mud-splattered, grinning, arms around each other's shoulders. A third figure was blurred in motion—a soldier walking by with a cigarette in his hand.

"That's him," Himmat said.

He handed the photo to Ruhan.

"Ravi died a week after this. Landmine. Harish blamed himself. He'd told Ravi to take that route. Swore he didn't see the signs."

Ruhan looked at the face of the man he had never known.

Ravi had sharp eyes. A scar down one cheek. And a half-smile like he knew more than he was letting on.

"Your grandfather stopped painting after that. At least out loud."

Himmat leaned back, staring at the ceiling like it owed him something.

"You think you know someone. And then they disappear. Or they leave you with only one side of the story."

Ruhan looked at the medal in the box. Bronze. Dusty.

It had Ravi's name etched faintly into the side.

"I think," Ruhan said slowly, "he carried the other side all his life."

Ruhan took the medal in his hands.

It was heavier than it looked. *Not by grams—by memory.*

The edges were dull, the engraving nearly worn. But it still held that strange, quiet dignity: the kind that doesn't announce itself, only remains.

He turned it over, then looked back at the photograph.

The way the men smiled. The way dirt clung to their uniforms was like a second skin. The way one of them—the blurred man—was halfway out of frame, but somehow still in the moment.

"Do you want to keep it?" Himmat asked.

Ruhan looked up. "The medal?"

"No. The truth."

The room seemed to inhale with the question.

Ruhan set the medal back gently, then reached into his satchel for his sketchbook.

"I'd like to draw you," he said.

Himmat arched a brow. "I'm not a monument, boy."

"No. But you are a memory."

That made the older man chuckle—a dry, sandpaper sound, unused to laughing.

He sat still.

And Ruhan began.

He started with the eyes.

Himmat's face was a cartography of experience—*folds like dry riverbeds, scars etched by time, a mouth that held stories behind its frowns.* Ruhan didn't idealize it. He didn't chase perfection. He *just...translated.*

As his hand moved, Himmat spoke.

"That morning, we thought it would rain."

The voice was softer now. Not for drama—for remembering.

"Harish was sketching again. He used to draw the hills. Called them bones of the earth. Ravi joked that he'd die before he ever drew a rifle."

"He wasn't wrong."

Ruhan didn't speak. *His pencil did.*

"Ravi was fast. Not just on foot—in life. Always first to speak. First to volunteer. First to take the longer route. That day, there were signs. Harish didn't see them. Or maybe he did, and trusted that Ravi would too."

"Landmines don't care what you see."

Himmat shifted slightly, but held still.

"It didn't tear him apart. Not physically. That's the lie people think. *It's neater than you'd expect. He was just...gone. In the space between two steps.*"

Ruhan paused his sketching.

"Did my grandfather ever talk to you about it? After?"

"Once."

A long silence.

"He came to me with a painting. It was of Ravi. But it didn't look like him. It looked like *grief pretending to smile.* I didn't take it. Told him to keep it."

"Do you regret that?"

Himmat didn't answer. Not with words.

But his gaze dropped.

The sketch began to take shape. Ruhan captured the coat—*not as it had once looked, but as it looked now—soft around the shoulders, stubborn at the collar, stitched through with history.* He shaded the medals faintly, suggesting their outline rather than screaming their presence.

When he was done, he turned the page around.

"It's not finished," he said.

Himmat studied it for a long time.

"***Neither am I.***"

They sat for a while in the silence.

"Do you know what peace feels like?" Himmat asked suddenly.

Ruhan shook his head.

"It's not relief. Not comfort. Its absence. *Peace is when everything finally shuts up.*"

"That letter...it didn't bring me peace."

"But it reminded me of the noise. And that's something."

As the afternoon light shifted, Ruhan stood to leave.

He handed the drawing to Himmat, who took it with more care than Ruhan expected.

"You'll be delivering more letters?" the old man asked.

"I think so," Ruhan replied. "They're...part of something I didn't know I was in."

"Then remember this."

Himmat looked him dead in the eye.

"Some stories are like landmines. Just because they've been buried doesn't mean they won't go off."

Ruhan nodded slowly.

He turned to go, but stopped at the threshold.

"Would you ever want the painting back?"

Himmat looked at the cabinet. Then at the sketch.

"I think I already have."

Outside, the sky had turned the colour of old bronze.

The walk to the station was long, but Ruhan didn't rush it. *He felt...full. Not with answers. With questions that mattered.*

The letter was delivered.

But something lingered.

Not guilt. Not regret.

Responsibility.

He took out his notebook and wrote a single line before the train arrived:

"Some faces don't fade. They wait until you know how to see them."

The train rocked gently as Ruhan sat by the window, the passing fields a blur of green and gold. He hadn't spoken much since boarding. He didn't need to. The letter had been delivered. The story had been heard.

But now...something was echoing inside him.

He kept seeing Himmat's face—not the real one, but the one he'd drawn. How the sketch didn't just show a man, but a weight. A lifetime of holding in. A survivor's silence, louder than grief.

He flipped open his notebook.

Under the line he had written earlier, he sketched again—this time from memory. Not the medal. Not the coat. Just eyes, worn and watching. They belonged to a man who had outlived too much and remembered it all.

Underneath, he scrawled:

"Not everything loud is said out loud."

When he returned to the house, it was dusk.

The ancestral home greeted him like it always did—not warmly, not coldly. Just there. Breathing in the corners.

He passed the living room. His father sat in silence, a file open on his lap, but his eyes distant—like he hadn't read a word.

Their gazes met, held for a second, then drifted apart.

No words. Just a nod. That strange, new ritual of theirs.

Ruhan moved past him and up the stairs.

The studio smelled like old paper and turpentine again. The box of letters still waited on the desk, untouched since he'd left.

He sat down slowly. The light from the window hit the desk at an angle that made the brass box glow faintly, as if it still held heat from all the emotions sealed inside.

He opened the sketchbook and placed today's drawing next to the earlier ones.

The room suddenly felt fuller.

Like it was watching him back.

He reached into the box again. This time, without fear.

He shuffled through until his fingers found a familiar one—"To My Son."

His breath hitched.

He wasn't ready. Still. But he could no longer pretend it wasn't calling him.

He didn't open it. Not yet.

He just placed one among them on the desk beside the others.

Looked at it. Let it exist.

He leaned back and closed his eyes.

And in that quiet, he imagined what these letters might say. Not the words, but the weight behind them.

Would it be full of apologies?

Or explanation?

Or worse—neither?

Something moved at the edge of his vision.

He turned.

A shadow? A breeze?

No. Just a memory—flickering behind his eyes.

He was nine. His grandfather had come back from a trip, sunburnt and tired. Ruhan had shown him a terrible drawing—two birds and a mountain that looked like a loaf of bread.

"You see too much," his grandfather had said with a smile. But you still don't know how to put it into words.

Back then, Ruhan thought it was a compliment.

Now he wasn't so sure.

He picked up a fresh page and began sketching again.

But this time, he didn't draw Himmat. Or the medal. Or his grandfather.

He drew himself.

Or tried to.

A boy holding a letter.

Behind him—shadows of faces, some angry, some sorrowful, some kind.

And around him—brushstrokes. Half-finished. Fading. Blurred.

It wasn't perfect.

But it was honest.

He folded the sketch in half and slid it into the box, beneath the rest.

Maybe someday, someone else would open it.

Maybe they'd understand him the way he was trying to understand all these strangers.

Maybe.

As the day dimmed, he whispered aloud—to the studio, to himself, to no one:

"I'm listening."

The next morning, the sky held a colour Ruhan couldn't quite name—not blue, not grey, but something in between. Like it hadn't made up its mind.

The world outside had already moved on. Milk carts rattled past. Someone down the road was hammering metal. The news played faintly from a neighbour's window.

But inside the studio, time hadn't started yet.

He sat at the desk, a cup of tea gone cold beside him, the box of letters closed again—not hidden, just resting. The sketchbook lay open to the self-portrait he'd made the night before.

He stared at it for a while.

Then, slowly, he tore it out.

Folded it in thirds.

Slid it into an envelope.

He scribbled a name and address:

"Himmat Singh. c/o Postmaster, Village Rampur, District Firozabad."

And beneath it, in small, careful letters:

"Thank you for the silence you've survived."

At the post office, he hesitated before handing it over.

The woman at the counter looked at him with mild impatience.

"Speed post?"

He shook his head.

"No rush."

The woman shrugged, stamped it, and tossed it in the tray behind her—where it vanished beneath a dozen other lives in transit.

Ruhan walked out feeling...not lighter. But less alone.

Back in the studio, a breeze had wandered in through the window.

The curtain fluttered slightly. One of the brushes on the desk rolled a few inches and stopped.

He picked up the letter again.

"To My Son."

His hands didn't shake this time.

But he still didn't open it.

Not yet.

Instead, he did something else.

He reached for a blank page.

Took a pen.

And began writing.

Not for anyone else. Not even for the future.

Just...to say something.

"To Whom It Never Reached—

I don't know who you are yet.

Maybe you're me. Maybe you're someone I've lost.

But if you ever find this—

Know that I am trying.

To listen.

To understand.

And maybe one day, to forgive."

He folded it carefully and slid it into the back of the brass box.

Not to forget.

But to join.

Because now he understood:

This wasn't just a collection of letters.

It was a choir.

Of regrets.

Of confessions.

Of truths too raw to say out loud.

And finally, finally—

Ruhan was singing back.

Chapter 6: The Lost Love

The morning light in the studio had a soft warmth—the kind that lingered, as if reluctant to disturb the dust.

Ruhan sat at the desk, with the brass box open before him once more.

It didn't feel like trespassing anymore.

It felt like restoration.

He reached in slowly, fingers brushing against the edges of familiar papers. He wasn't looking for anything in particular. But sometimes, the right things find you when you stop searching.

His hand closed around a thinner sheet. The paper was older, more delicate, folded with a reverence he hadn't found in others.

There was no envelope. Just a name.

"Lilavati."

He paused.

The script was different this time—still his grandfather's, but softer. Like he had written it slowly, with a kind of care that feared its own weight.

Ruhan unfolded the letter.

"Lilavati,"

"If I had one evening left in this life, I would spend it in silence beside you."

"Not to speak. Not to explain. Just to sit with all that was unsaid between us."

"You always said silence was your favourite colour. I never understood that, until I tried to live without you."

The words blurred for a second.

Ruhan blinked.

This wasn't like the others.

This wasn't regret that burned.

This was love that lingered.

"We made the right decision. I know that."

"But some decisions are made in quiet places where right and wrong speak different languages."

"I hope you found joy. I hope someone loved you the way I couldn't—fully, publicly, without apology."

"But know this—in every painting I never signed, in every sky I left unshaded, you are there."

"Still the softest blue I've ever known."

"Still the silence I would have chosen, if the world had let me."

"Yours in every unframed memory,"

"Harish."

Ruhan sat still for a long while.

Something about the letter didn't feel like the others.

It wasn't written to be forgiven. Or to be resolved.

It was written to remember.

He refolded the letter and set it gently on the desk.

A name like Lilavati didn't fade. It lingered in paintings, old letters, and maybe—just maybe—in places the world forgot to look—old studios, dusty shelves, and quiet corners of memory.

He didn't know what he expected to feel.

Jealousy? No.

Confusion? A little.

But mostly, he felt tenderness. For a man who had loved, and lost, and chosen silence over the theatre of grief.

And he couldn't help but wonder—

Had his grandfather ever told anyone about her?

Had he ever tried to find her again?

And more hauntingly—

Would Ruhan have made the same choice?

He looked at his phone. No signal in the old house.

But that wasn't going to stop him.

He stood slowly, pressed the letter into a careful fold, sealed it inside the protective folder, and carried it with him down the stairs.

His father was in the courtyard, pruning the bougainvillea that never listened.

"Did Dadu ever mention someone named Lilavati?" Ruhan asked.

His father didn't look up right away.

"Once. A long time ago."

"What did he say?"

A pause.

"That he almost loved her. But it was a time when 'almost' had to be enough."

Ruhan waited, but that was all his father offered.

Almost.

It always circled back to that word, didn't it?

Later that afternoon, Ruhan sat in the town library.

The building still smelled like varnish and old ambition.

He flipped through community records, scrapbooks, festival rosters. Something about the name Lilavati pulled him.

And then he saw it.

A photograph—grainy, faded—of a woman beside a veena, in a cultural magazine from decades ago.

Lilavati A. Desai. Retired music teacher.

Resides in a quiet house near the temple road in Bhavnagar.

Bhavnagar.

Not far.

Ruhan closed the book gently, his heart slightly unsteady.

He had no plan.

But maybe, *that's how all-important stories began.*

The house sat at the end of a quiet lane, wrapped in the kind of silence that felt chosen, not abandoned. A rusted wind chime stirred gently above the gate. Jasmine crept along the compound wall like it had been growing for years without interruption.

Ruhan stood outside for a long time before ringing the bell.

A soft ting echoed inside.

For a moment, nothing.

Then slow footsteps. A pause.

And finally, the door creaked open.

She stood framed in the light—Lilavati, aged gracefully into a woman who looked like she had lived without rushing. Her silver hair was pinned back in a careful braid, her sari cotton and sun-fadedworn. There was no makeup. No pretence.

Just stillness.

And eyes that once must've held music.

"Yes?" she asked.

Ruhan smiled politely, unsure of the right introduction.

"I...I'm Ruhan. Harishbhai's grandson."

The name hit like a soft ripple in still water.

Her eyes shifted. Not in fear. But recognition.

"You look like him," she said gently. "But your silence sounds different."

He blinked. That was not what he expected.

"May I...come in? Just for a few minutes. There's something I'd like to show you."

She led him into a modest living room. Cushions softened from years of use. Shelves with books, mostly poetry. A veena rested in the corner, its strings silent but not forgotten.

She made tea without asking.

Ruhan waited until the tray was placed between them before gently pulling out the folder.

He slid it across the table.

"I found this in his studio. Among other letters. He never sent it."

Lilavati didn't rush to open it. She simply rested her hand on the folder.

"I knew he had written it. I just didn't know it still existed."

"He told you?"

"No. But we were both the kind of people who said our goodbyes with letters we never mailed."

She opened it slowly.

And read in silence.

Ruhan didn't interrupt.

He studied her hands as they held the paper—trembling slightly, but not from weakness.

When she finished, she folded the letter again. Not tightly. Not with anger.

But with care. As if preserving something she'd already forgiven.

“He was always softer in writing,” she said.

“You knew him well?”

She smiled—that kind of smile only the very old and the very honest manage.

“I knew a version of him. The one who danced between decisions and never learned how to stop in the middle. We were...almost something.”

“Why didn't it happen?”

She looked out the window before answering.

“He had responsibilities. I had pride. And the world didn't offer many options to those who wanted love without scandal.”

A breeze stirred through the curtains.

Ruhan swallowed the question that burned in his throat—Was it worth it?

Instead, he asked—

“Do you regret it?”

Lilavati considered the question, then shook her head slowly.

“No. I regret nothing. But I miss...the possibility of what could've been.”

There was silence for a while.

The tea cooled. The shadows shifted.

And then Lilavati reached for a book from the nearby shelf.

It was old—the spine cracked, the cover plain.

She opened to a marked page and slid it toward Ruhan.

A single verse had been underlined in red.

"Some loves do not ask for forever.

They only ask to be remembered kindly."

He looked up.

She met his gaze.

"That's all he ever asked. And I have."

Ruhan stood to leave a few minutes later.

He didn't want to intrude further.

But before he stepped out, he turned one last time.

"He never stopped painting."

"I know," she said.

"I think...you were in every sky."

She smiled again—wider this time, though her eyes shone with the kind of grief that had aged well.

"Tell him thank you, if you find him in yourself someday."

"I think I'm trying," Ruhan said softly.

Back on the street, the world felt heavier.

Not because of sorrow. But because of the truth.

That love—real, messy, unfinished love—didn't always fit neatly into stories.

Sometimes it just lives quietly, in the background of everything else.

And sometimes, it still waits in jasmine-scented homes on quiet lanes.

That night, in his studio, Ruhan drew again.

A woman seated beside a veena, sunlight falling on her face.

And behind her, through an open window, a sky washed in the softest blue.

Back in the studio, night had fallen with a kind of hush. The kind that settles after something unnameable has shifted.

Ruhan placed the sketch beside his teacup, watching the charcoal smudge across the woman's cheek in a way that almost looked like a tear. He didn't try to fix it.

He let it be.

Some stories were not meant to be perfected, only remembered. He opened the brass box again. The letters inside looked the same. But he didn't. *Something inside him had changed—quietly, like roots breaking through softened ground.*

He pulled out the letter to Lilavati once more. Read it slowly, tracing each word as if it were a fingerprint. His grandfather had never intended to send it, yet it carried the weight of an unspoken lifetime.

A kind of bravery, Ruhan wasn't sure he had in him yet.

He stared at the pile of unopened letters.

And wondered—

Would he ever write one of his own?

Later that night, he found himself on the terrace.

The stars were faint behind the street lamps and power lines. But they were still there.

He thought of Lilavati, sitting in her quiet home with her veena and her jasmine vines, folding the letter with the grace of someone who had long made peace with her ghosts.

She hadn't needed closure. She had built a life beside the absence, not against it.

Could he?

Ruhan rubbed his hands together—cold despite the humid night—and then opened his notebook.

It had been days since he wrote anything that belonged only to him.

He didn't think.

He just began.

"Dear Almost,"

"I don't know who you are yet. Maybe I met you already. Maybe I ran from you.

But today, I learned something about love—that it doesn't always need a future to have mattered."

"And maybe the bravest thing is not falling in love. It's allowing yourself to remember it kindly."

He didn't sign it.

Didn't fold it.

Just let it live there, on the page, a quiet truth.

He slipped the notebook back under his pillow.

And lay down, eyes open to a ceiling he'd stared at hundreds of times before—but tonight, it didn't press down on him. In the morning, he woke earlier than usual.

The light in the studio felt different again—not softer, not warmer, but clearer.

Ruhan picked up the sketch of Lilavati once more.

He turned it over and wrote on the back:

"Some skies never fade. Some names remain, even in silence."

He didn't know what he'd do with it. Not yet.

Maybe frame it.

Maybe send it.

Maybe simply keep it tucked between the pages of something else—a secret that didn't want to be hidden, only protected.

That afternoon, as he stood by the box again, he picked up another letter at random.

This one was addressed simply:

"To Devika"

He didn't recognize the name.

But a strange feeling crept in—not dread, not excitement.

Curiosity that beat like a pulse.

He wasn't ready to read it yet.

But he would.

Soon.

Chapter 7: Shadows of the Past

The rain had finally stopped.

Outside, the trees dripped with relief, and the studio's open window let in a breeze that smelled of damp earth and something forgotten—*like the past had been stirred awake.*

Ruhan sat at the desk again, the brass box beside him. His tea had gone cold.

He wasn't reading the letters in order anymore. He had given up trying to control the rhythm of memory. Now, he let the letters find him.

He reached in, pulling one from the lower stack. Its fold was uneven. The ink had bled through the edges.

It was addressed to:

"Devendra Patel"

The name rang no bell.

The handwriting was slightly harsher this time—more rushed, more weighted. *Like the pen itself had protested.*

Ruhan unfolded it carefully. A cold shiver ran down his arms before he'd even begun to read.

"Devendra,"

"You trusted me, and I made that trust into a currency I spent in silence."

"I've told myself, for years, that I had no choice. That I acted out of obligation. But maybe that's what cowardice looks like when you frame it in self-righteousness."

"Your land should have been yours. That studio space...the one where my grandson now paints...it belonged to you once. Until I signed the paper."

"You asked me not to. And I did."

"And every time I walked through that gate, I wondered if you could hear it too—the betrayal in the hinges."

Ruhan sat up straighter.

His fingers tightened.

The studio?

This studio?

He kept reading.

"The man who asked me to sign was not evil. He was practical. Promised employment. A better road. A cleaner divide.

I signed because I thought I was choosing progress.

But I never asked you what it cost you."

"I heard you moved your family to a smaller place. That your wife fell ill. That your daughter never forgave the neighbourhood."

"I never asked if it was true. I never had the courage."

"You once said: **'The difference between a thief and a traitor is which way they're facing when they leave.'**

I've been walking backwards for years."

By the time he reached the final line, Ruhan couldn't feel his fingers.

His eyes scanned the room—the very room that now throbbed with unspoken grief.

The wooden beams above him. The corner where his grandfather's easel once stood. The same floor where he had sat cross-legged as a boy.

This place had always felt sacred.

Now it felt...borrowed, maybe even stolen.

He set the letter down slowly.

The silence in the studio no longer felt sacred.

It felt complicit.

He stood, restless. His heart was loud in his ears. He needed answers, or air—maybe both.

He grabbed the letter, folded it back into its aged creases, and walked downstairs.

Radhika—little more than a passing name in his childhood—was in the living room now, folding old shawls with quiet precision that felt almost foreign to him.

"Bua," he said, his voice quieter than he expected. "Do you remember anyone named Devendra Patel?"

She didn't look up at first.

Then she stilled.

"Why are you asking about Devendra?"

"There's a letter. From Dadu. It...it says something about this house. About land that wasn't his to begin with."

Radhika exhaled through her nose.

"It was never a secret," she said. **"Just a wound we didn't dress in public."**

She sat down, the folded shawls now forgotten.

"Devendra was our neighbour. A good man. Honest. He and your grandfather argued over the property line for years. Then one day, a document arrived, and your grandfather signed it."

"Without telling him?"

"They'd argued—many times. Your Dada believed the municipality was backing the deal. But yes, he knew what it meant. He knew Devendra would lose his portion."

"Why did he do it?"

Radhika looked at Ruhan, eyes tired.

"He thought he was protecting us. We were struggling. The studio was at risk. He told himself it was the lesser evil."

"Did Papa know?"

She nodded.

"He never forgave him for it. That's when the silence between them began. Not when your mother left. Before that."

Ruhan leaned against the wall, suddenly cold.

All this time, he thought the letters were about redemption.

He hadn't realized some were about guilt.

Real, lasting guilt.

And he hadn't realized that the fractures in his family didn't start with him—they started with choices.

Back in the studio, Ruhan sat again.

The room looked the same.

But nothing felt untouched anymore.

He pulled out his sketchbook and stared at the blank page.

He didn't draw.

He wrote:

"What do you do when the hands that raised you once took something that wasn't theirs?"

"And what do you do when you're still using it to build your truth?"

He let the silence answer for him.

He just let the questions hang.

The next morning was overcast again, as if the sky itself had gone back to grieving.

Ruhan couldn't sit still.

There was a hollowness in his chest that wouldn't go away—*the kind that came not from pain, but from disorientation.* He wasn't just uncovering memories anymore. He was unearthing consequences.

He had to know more.

A quick online search brought up a narrow lead—a listing under the name Siddharth D. Patel, architect, registered at an address across town.

It was a long shot.

But something told him the "D" stood for Devendra.

The apartment complex was modest. Not old, but weary—as if it had settled for a kind of silence that demanded nothing but maintenance.

He rang the bell.

Footsteps approached.

The door opened to reveal a man in his late thirties. He had his grandfather's sadness in his eyes, but none of the softness.

"Yes?"

"Hi," Ruhan said. "I'm...sorry to come unannounced. I'm Ruhan Desai. My grandfather was Harish Desai."

The name dropped like a stone in still water.

Siddharth's jaw clenched.

His shoulders stiffened.

"And?"

"I found something. A letter. Written to your father. From mine."

Silence.

"He never sent it," Ruhan added.

Siddharth looked past him, as if debating whether to shut the door or not.

Then, slowly, he opened it wider.

"You better come in."

The living room was neat. Functional. Books on architecture. A few awards on the shelf. And yet—no photographs. No clutter. Nothing that made it feel inherited.

"My father passed away four years ago," Siddharth said, sitting down across from him. "Lung complications. He was a quiet man by the end. Still angry. But quiet."

Ruhan hesitated, then pulled out the letter.

Siddharth didn't reach for it.

Not immediately.

"He used to mutter your grandfather's name sometimes," he said. "Whenever the rent increased. Or when we'd pass the old neighbourhood. I never understood the full story."

"I didn't either," Ruhan admitted. "Until yesterday."

He offered the letter again.

Siddharth took it this time.

Read it silently, the weight in his brows deepening line by line.

When he was done, he folded it once, then again—tighter than necessary.

"It would've meant more if he'd sent it when it mattered."

Ruhan nodded.

"I know."

"But..." Siddharth sighed. "It's strange, isn't it? That even silence ages."

They sat in stillness for a few moments.

"My father wasn't ruined by what happened," Siddharth said eventually. "But he was changed. The displacement—it taught him never to trust kindness without a signature."

"Do you blame my grandfather?"

Siddharth looked at him. Not harshly.

"I don't know him enough to blame. But I know enough not to forget."

Ruhan swallowed the guilt sitting at the back of his throat.

"Do you want to keep the letter?"

"No," Siddharth said. "It belongs to the past. And to you."

"He wanted to apologize."

"Then maybe it's your turn now."

That landed like a truth Ruhan wasn't ready for—but couldn't deny.

Back at home, Ruhan opened his sketchbook again.

No drawings.

Just words.

"Today, I met the echo of a wound I never knew I inherited.

It didn't scream. It didn't accuse. It simply existed—waiting to be acknowledged."

He closed the book, then picked up a blank postcard from his drawer.

He didn't know where he'd send it.

Or if he'd send it at all.

But he wrote:

Dear Siddharth,

You didn't ask for it. But I'm sorry.

For the roof I inherited. For the silence you did. And for the way we were both raised under shadows that didn't belong to us.

I hope the ceilings you build are lighter than the ones you've lived under.

He left it unsigned.

That evening, as the light slipped into gold, softening the edges of everything it touched, Ruhan returned to the studio.

He stood at the doorway for a long time—not entering, just listening.

As if the walls had something left to confess.

The studio door creaked as Ruhan stepped inside.

It wasn't haunted. Not exactly.

But it was no longer weightless either.

He had always thought of it as a space of creation—now he understood it was also a space of inheritance. And **inheritance, he was learning, wasn't just legacy. It was debt.**

He sat by the window, where the evening light painted long shadows across the floor.

The letter to Devendra Patel lay open again. This time, it didn't surprise him. It hurt less—but in the way a healed scar itches when touched. *A reminder. A residue.*

He found himself thinking about his father again.

What it must've been like to grow up in this same house, knowing your father had hurt someone and never spoken of it. What it must've done to a boy raised by silence.

Maybe it explained the distance between them—*not built in anger, but in disappointment.* In unspoken things that hung too long in the air.

Later that night, Ruhan wandered downstairs. The house was dim, quiet, holding its breath like it always did after dark.

He found his father in the backyard as the last of the light faded, tending to the hibiscus that had survived despite years of neglect.

"The red ones bloomed early this year," his father said without turning.

"I don't remember them blooming at all."

"That's because they used to get plucked before you saw them."

Ruhan smiled faintly, though his heart was full of static.

"Can I ask you something?" he said.

"You already are."

"Devendra Patel. You knew what happened, right?"

His father's hands froze on the hose.

A long pause followed. Not heavy. Just inevitable.

"I knew," he said finally. "I was sixteen. I saw him the day the land was measured. I knew what it meant before anyone said a word."

"Why didn't you ever...talk about it?"

His father looked up at the moon—barely a slice in the sky.

"Because there's a difference between forgiving and forgetting. And I never managed either."

"But he regretted it," Ruhan offered. "He wrote him a letter."

"Which he never sent."

There was no anger in his voice. Nothing but weariness.

"Your grandfather was a good man, Ruhan. But not a flawless one. I worshipped him when I was a boy. And when I found out the truth...I didn't know how to love him and question him at the same time."

"I think I know what that feels like," Ruhan said.

A breeze passed between them. Small. Kind.

They stood in silence.

But *it wasn't the old silence. It wasn't avoidance. It wasn't punishment.*

It was something closer to recognition.

Back in the studio, Ruhan sketched for the first time in days.

Not a face.

Not a place.

Just shadows—the way they stretched along floorboards, the way they bent around boxes and corners. The way they existed, sustained only by light.

At the bottom of the page, he wrote:

"He was human. I have to make peace with that—or I'll never forgive myself for being human too."

He picked up the postcard again.

Read the apology he'd written to Siddharth.

Then turned it over and, for the first time, wrote a name in the corner:

Ruhan.

Not as an artist.

Not as a grandson.

Just...a person trying to do the right thing.

He left it on the studio desk.

Beside the brass box.

And didn't look back as he turned off the light.

Chapter 8: The Apology to His Son

The morning light came soft and indifferent, sliding across the floor of the studio *like it had no knowledge of the night that passed.* Ruhan hadn't slept. Not truly. His eyes had closed, yes—but his mind never surrendered. The previous letter, the story of Lilavati and Harish, still lingered in the corners of the room like the scent of old jasmine—sweet and aching.

He sat cross-legged on the floor, the box of letters beside him, its lid half open *like a mouth mid-sentence.* He reached for the next envelope without ceremony.

But when he saw the name on it, his hand paused mid-air.

"To My Son"

Not a name. Just...that.

His chest tightened instantly. His fingers hovered over it like the letter itself might burn. There had been letters to lovers, to friends, to strangers—some to ghosts. But this one... this one felt like it belonged to another realm altogether. A letter not just from his grandfather—but one addressed to his father.

And *perhaps, in some sideways, aching way—also to him.*

His first instinct was to put it back. Bury it. Walk away. Pretend he never saw it.

But curiosity, that quiet beast that lived in the corners of grief, pushed him forward.

He took a breath and unfolded the letter.

The first words blurred. His eyes moved across the lines, but the meaning lagged.

“To My Son,

I do not know if this letter will ever reach you.

I am not writing it for that.

I am writing it because my hands cannot bear the weight of all the things I never said.”

Ruhan stopped reading.

The paper trembled in his hands, but he wasn’t sure if it was the wind—or him.

He stood abruptly, pacing across the room before walking to the window and pulling it open. The studio air felt too full. Too many memories. Too many ghosts. The silence was louder than ever.

Outside, a school bell rang in the distance. Children’s laughter spilled into the air. It felt...impossible. How could the world be laughing while letters like these existed?

He returned to the letter—slower this time. Like someone touching a scar.

“I have loved you in a way I never learned how to show.

When you were small, you clung to me like I was the whole sky.

And when you grew up, you looked at me like I was the wall you needed to break.

Perhaps I was both. And perhaps I was wrong."

Ruhan closed his eyes. He could feel his grandfather in these lines—not the stern old man in the chair, but a man unravelling decades of silence in ink.

He thought of his father—not the man who sat wordless at the dining table now, but the one who once carved him a wooden bird when he was seven. He remembered how he'd dropped it accidentally, breaking its wing. His father hadn't shouted. Just picked it up and placed it in a drawer.

It was never seen again.

No confrontation. No explanation. Just...vanishing. *That's how it always was. With emotions. With closeness. With him.*

And yet, here were letters. *A breath from the past. A wound, still open, still bleeding across generations.*

He placed the first letter addressed "To My Son", gently on the desk and sat beside it—not to read, but to simply be near it. It was strange how a piece of paper could feel heavier than years of silence.

He poured a glass of water. Drank half. Then returned.

"I have failed you in the quiet ways.

Not in the ways people write books about—

But in the ones only you would carry.

When your mother died, I died too, a little.

I became something smaller. Something quieter.

You needed a father.

But I gave you a ghost.

I am sorry for that."

Ruhan blinked. Hard. His throat closed around a truth he didn't know he had been storing for years.

Yes, after his mother died, his father had become more machine than man. Every smile looked like a cracked mirror—dangerous to hold. Every silence, a wall that grew taller.

Ruhan had hated him for it.

And now...this letter made him wonder if Harish had hated himself, too.

This wasn't just an apology—it was a revelation.

It was a man admitting he had been lost, and in the process, had led his son into the same maze.

Ruhan laid the letter flat, smoothing out the creases with his palm *as if he could undo time by making the paper straight again.* His eyes lingered on a line near the bottom of the page.

"You grew into a man without my guidance,

And **I punished you for growing in ways I didn't understand.**

I wish I had told you that I was proud of you.

I wish I had told you that **your silence was not your fault—**

It was mine, reflected in you."

He ran a hand over his face.

Was it possible for a man to destroy someone quietly? Without raised voices or broken plates—just absence?

The silence between his father and his grandfather had been an inheritance. Passed on like *a curse dressed as dignity.* Now he saw it for what it truly was—*grief wearing pride as a mask.*

Ruhan felt like he was standing at the edge of something—*an unravelling, perhaps. Or a beginning.*

He remembered something strange. A moment from childhood: he had asked his father, "Do you think I'll be like you when I grow up?" And his father had said, after a pause, "I hope not."

At the time, Ruhan had taken it as a rejection.

But now, maybe...it was a warning.

He turned the page. There was more.

"This letter is not forgiveness.

It is not even redemption.

It is a wound, spoken aloud—so that maybe it won't be carried further.

If you ever read this, know this:

I loved you.

In every way, I failed to say.

And in every way, I still don't know how."

Ruhan let the letter fall into his lap.

No signature.

No neat farewell.

Just that final line. A full stop at the end of a life's apology.

He looked out the window again. The children were gone. The street is quiet. The light is sharper now.

He folded the letter slowly, with reverence, and placed it back in the envelope. It felt wrong to keep it, but also wrong to destroy it. Like it belonged somewhere sacred.

For a long while, he just sat there. No music. No tears. *Just breath, paper, and the weight of something lifting and something landing—simultaneously.*

Later that evening, he found his father sitting outside, trimming the edges of a bush that didn't need trimming.

Ruhan sat beside him in silence.

For the first time in years, it wasn't uncomfortable.

He wanted to speak. He didn't. Not yet. But he did *something smaller. Something quieter.*

He passed the envelope to him.

His father took it. Didn't ask anything. His fingers lingered on the name—"To My Son."

He didn't open it then. Just held it.

And maybe that was enough—for now.

That night, sleep didn't come easily to Ruhan.

But when it did, it came soft and dreamless—*like the body finally trusted the world enough to rest.*

By morning, the envelope was no longer on the table, leaving behind only the neat square of cleared dust where it had rested.

And though no words had been spoken between them, **some silence had shifted.**

It no longer hurts to carry.

It began to hold the possibility of something else.

Something like peace.

Chapter 9: "The Stranger"

The letter was unlike anything Ruhan had ever read.

Its paper, yellowed and brittle, had been folded more times than seemed necessary—creased as if it had been opened and closed in hesitation, over and over again. The ink had bled faintly in places, a testament to time, or perhaps to the trembling hands of its writer. This one didn't begin with "My dear," or "To you." It had no name at all. Just one line:

"I still see your eyes when I close mine."

Ruhan stared at it, feeling a strange discomfort creep into his chest. There was no other preamble—only a date from decades ago, and then, a confession that felt more like a wound than a memory.

"That day on the riverbank...I should've stopped. I should've listened to your side before speaking mine. But I was young. And proud. And I let my anger ruin what mattered. I knew I had broken something that wouldn't heal. Yet I lived on, pretending the silence was enough punishment. It wasn't."

Ruhan didn't know who this man was. There was no name at the end either. Only a final line, haunting in its stillness:

"If this letter ever finds its way to you—I'm sorry."

That was it.

No return address. No recipient. No clue—except a barely legible watermark from a guesthouse in Bhuj.

He could have put it away. Label it as a lost cause, a story too fragmented to follow. But something in it gnawed at him—like a riddle meant for him, *like a stranger looking at him from across time, asking to be found.*

And so, with the kind of stubbornness that had started to feel like purpose, Ruhan boarded a bus to Bhuj the next morning.

Bhuj was dust and heat. Even in February, the sun pressed down like a weight, and the wind that came off the salt desert offered little relief. The town was old—not in the proud, showy way, but quietly. Its cracks weren't painted over; its silence wasn't filled with performance. It simply was...

Ruhan stepped off the bus with the letter in his pocket, a water bottle in his bag, and no idea where to begin.

The guesthouse mentioned in the watermark—Shyam Niwas—still existed. But barely.

A hunched old man sat at the front, chewing betel leaves and spitting into a rusted tin can. His eyes narrowed when Ruhan mentioned the letter.

"Who are you looking for?" he asked.

"I don't know his name," Ruhan admitted, "but this letter came from here. Decades ago."

The old man stared at him, unblinking. "And you think he still lives?"

"I don't know," Ruhan said again. "But maybe someone remembers him."

There was a long pause before the man scratched his chin and pointed to the back lane. "Try the library. *People don't forget much in books.*"

The library was small and dark, its air thick with the scent of yellowing pages and old rugs. A woman in her seventies greeted him with wary kindness. When he explained his quest, she listened patiently.

"A man who wrote a letter but didn't sign it?" she repeated.

"Yes."

She disappeared behind a curtain of shelves and returned with a register older than his father. "We had a writing workshop here," she said. "Long ago. People wrote things they never meant to send. Some wrote to their past. Some to their guilt. A few...never even showed up again."

She flipped the pages, slowly, carefully.

There it was.

Entry: Harish Desai–1989.

Ruhan blinked. *The name felt like thunder in his skull.*

Harish Desai—his grandfather.

He stared at the register, at the familiar handwriting. A note beside the name read: "Wrote a letter. Didn't read it aloud. Left early."

"Do you know who the letter was for?" Ruhan whispered.

The librarian shook her head. "But he handed it to someone. A man who came every week. Quiet man. Lost a son. Name was Karsanbhai."

It took Ruhan another full day to trace Karsanbhai.

He didn't live in Bhuj anymore, but the tea stall vendor remembered him. Gave Ruhan the address of his son, who still ran a cotton shop in Mandvi, a town by the sea. So, Ruhan took another bus. Hours passed with the roads winding through dry lands and fleeting mirages.

He found the shop in the evening.

It was modest, tucked between two goldsmiths. A boy with eyes like a hawk and hair slicked back too neatly was at the counter. When Ruhan asked for Karsanbhai, the boy hesitated.

"He doesn't talk much now," the boy said. "He's old. Mostly sits by the beach."

"I need to speak with him," Ruhan said softly. "It's about a letter."

Ruhan noticed a man on a wooden bench, gazing out at the horizon with a patience that seemed unending.

He was thin, his back curved with age, but his eyes were alert and unclouded. Ruhan introduced himself and showed the letter. The moment Karsanbhai's eyes fell on it, something in his face shifted.

"I remember this paper," he murmured. "Your grandfather gave it to me. Said he couldn't bear to carry it anymore."

"Do you know who it was for?"

There was a long silence before the old man spoke again.

"My brother," he said. "Jasmat. They were friends. Business partners, almost like family."

"And something went wrong?"

Karsanbhai looked at Ruhan. "Your grandfather accused him of betrayal. A deal gone wrong. Money vanished. He confronted him there, on the riverbank. Words were said that should never be said. My brother left town that night. Never returned."

He paused. "Years later, Harish came to me. Gave me this letter. Asked me to find Jasmat. But I never did. I failed both of them."

Ruhan felt the weight of it settle in his chest.

"I want to find him," Ruhan said. "I want to give this letter to the one it was meant for."

Karsanbhai looked away, toward the sea, as if searching the horizon for a version of the past that still made sense.

"Then go to Anand," he said. "There's a temple there—he used to go. Maybe someone there still remembers his name."

At the edge of yet another town, Ruhan paused, feeling the weight of beginnings repeating themselves. This journey was no longer just about a letter. It had become a mirror—reflecting his own questions, his own inherited silences. *Every step he took for Harish felt like a step into his own shadows.* Every letter unearthed pulled him closer to stories left half-told.

He reached the temple at dusk. The air smelled of marigolds and sandalwood. Bells echoed from within, carried by the wind like faint voices.

He approached an old priest, who listened quietly to the story.

"Jasmat Bhai?" the priest said. "He used to come every full moon. Sat under the peepal tree. Talked a little. Prayed a lot."

"Is he still alive?" Ruhan asked.

The priest nodded slowly. "He lives just behind the temple. Still keeps silence. But maybe...today, he will speak."

Ruhan walked toward the back of the temple where the peepal tree stood wide and still, like an ancient keeper of time. A small stone path curved around it, leading to a modest house with whitewashed walls and a wooden door, faded and chipped. The yard was quiet. No lights on, but the faint sound of a radio hummed through the air, barely audible—a song from the sixties, melancholic and distant.

He stood there for a moment, hesitant. Then he knocked.

Nothing.

Another knock.

Still silence.

Ruhan turned to leave—when the door creaked open.

A man stood behind it, thinner than the outline the priest had described. His hair was snow-white, combed neatly back. He wore a simple kurta, and his eyes—though cloudy—carried a sharpness that made Ruhan straighten.

"Are you...Jasmat Bhai?" he asked, quietly.

The man didn't answer. He looked at Ruhan the way someone might look at a photograph of themselves from another life. With confusion. Recognition. And pain.

Ruhan reached into his pocket. "I think this...was written for you. Decades ago."

He unfolded the letter and handed it over.

Jasmat didn't touch it.

His eyes narrowed on the paper. As if he already knew what it was. As if the sight of it was a wound reopened.

"I have no need for ghosts," he said, his voice coarse but calm.

"I'm not here for ghosts," Ruhan replied gently. "I'm here because someone didn't know how to ask for forgiveness. And someone else didn't know how to hear it. But maybe...if you read this, both might find a little peace."

Jasmat stared at him.

And then, with a slow, trembling hand, he reached for the letter.

He didn't read it aloud. He didn't speak. He just stood in the doorway, unmoving, for minutes that felt like hours.

Ruhan watched the man's expression shift—at first unreadable, then softening into something between grief and release.

When he finally looked up, his voice cracked.

"Harish wrote this?"

"Yes," Ruhan nodded. "He was my grandfather."

Jasmat sat down on the doorstep, slowly, like the weight of the paper had turned his knees to ash.

"I waited for this," he whispered. "For so many years, I thought I'd imagined the look on his face that day. The regret. But he never came. Never wrote. Not until now."

He folded the letter back carefully, as if it were a relic.

"I left everything that night," Jasmat continued. "Not just the business. My dignity. My name. It was easier to disappear than to explain. He didn't believe me. And I didn't know how to defend myself against someone who already saw me guilty."

He looked at Ruhan again. "I lost my best friend."

There was a pause. Then Ruhan sat beside him.

"I lost mine too," he said quietly. "A few years ago."

They didn't speak for a while. The peepal leaves rustled gently, like *a lullaby meant only for two broken men beneath them.*

As the sun dipped behind the trees, Jasmat lit a small diya at the edge of his courtyard. "I don't believe in second chances," he said, "but I believe in closure."

He handed Ruhan the letter back.

"No," Ruhan said, refusing. "It was meant for you."

Jasmat looked at the paper, held it for a second longer, and then set it down inside the diya's flame.

Ruhan panicked. "Wait—"

But Jasmat only watched the fire.

"I've carried its silence long enough," he said. "**Let me return it to the wind.**"

The paper curled and turned black, then vanished, leaving only ash in its place.

That night, Ruhan didn't go back to his hotel.

He sat with Jasmat under the peepal tree, sipping warm chai that the old man had brewed. They spoke about everything and nothing—music, trees, regrets, and old radio shows.

"I never married," Jasmat said. "I couldn't. The silence had taken too much space inside me."

"I think silence is inherited," Ruhan murmured. "My father barely speaks. My grandfather wrote to strangers but not to his own family. And I..."

He hesitated.

"You write?" Jasmat asked.

Ruhan nodded. "Unsent letters. Like his."

Jasmat chuckled faintly. "Maybe it runs in the blood."

And then, softly, he said, "Thank you for finding me."

Ruhan carried those words with him into the silence of the night.

As he walked down the temple steps, he felt something shift inside him. Not an answer. Not a conclusion. But a loosening. A breath that no longer got caught in his ribs. He thought of Harish—not as the strong, silent man he'd remembered, but as someone who had once been fragile too. Someone who had been wrong. Who had loved, and failed, and still tried to make it right, even if too late.

He thought of all the stories buried inside his own family. The ones locked in letters, the ones burned before they were ever read.

And suddenly, it didn't feel strange that he was on this path. **It felt necessary.**

He walked into the morning sun, a new letter already forming in his head—not from the past this time, but for it. For his father. For himself.

When Ruhan left the next morning, Jasmat remained at the threshold, as if rooted there. Framed by the light of dawn—an old man weathered not just by time, but by truths too long unspoken. He didn't wave, but nodded. A soft, dignified gesture that felt more intimate than words.

Ruhan nodded back, a quiet smile forming. And for a moment, they both just stood there—two men from different ends of a story that had waited too long to be finished.

He took the road downhill, each step lighter than the one before.

A stranger had opened a door to the past, and somehow, it had unlatched a part of the future too.

Some stories, he realized, aren't told to undo the past—they're told so that another beginning, somewhere else, can take root. And for the first time in a long time, Ruhan didn't feel like he was running from anything.

He was walking toward something.

A silence that didn't ache anymore.

A name that no longer felt like a wound.

A letter, no longer unsent.

Chapter 10: The Woman Who Left

He hadn't planned on opening any more letters that week.

Bhuj, Mandvi, Jasmat—the long detour through old geography and older regret had left something tender exposed in him. Back home, he meant to rest. Sketch. Sit with what he'd learned. Maybe even ask his father about the garden soil like ordinary sons do.

But the box never really slept.

On his second morning back, while sorting the letters into rough piles—delivered, read, pending—a small, folded sheet slipped free and fluttered to the floor. Not one of the heavier, cream-stock pages. This was thin, almost translucent. Stationery paper. Something written fast, folded once, then again, tucked where it could be forgotten.

It wasn't addressed formally.

Just a line, in Harish's hand:

"For Meera—if you ever come back."

Ruhan froze.

He didn't remember seeing this before.

He unfolded it.

There was barely any ink on the inside, only four short sentences, spaced like breath.

"You left before I answered. That was my fault."

"The painting was always yours; I kept the silence, not the canvas."

"If you come back, tell me what remained."

—H

No date. No address. No clue who Meera was.

But painting. That word flared.

Ruhan scanned the studio—the unfinished canvases, the rolled ones in the corner; the stack in the storage rack wrapped in muslin. Have you ever carried something that wasn't originally yours? Had Harish promised it—and never delivered? Or delivered and taken it back?

He refolded the note and slipped it into his pocket.

He went downstairs to find Radhika in the courtyard sunning papads on a reed mat.

"Bua," he said carefully, "did Dadu ever mention someone named Meera?"

Radhika didn't answer right away. She pressed a bubble from the dough with two fingers, eyes narrowed against the light.

"Meera Vyas?" she said at last.

"You know her?"

"Everyone knew Meera. She ran the travelling arts programme—schools, hospitals, village murals. Your Dada donated paint. Then...something happened. She left midway through the city mural project and never returned."

"Did they—" He hesitated. "Were they close?"

Radhika gave him a look that older women reserve for the very young. "Close is a lazy word. They admired each other. She pushed him. He listened—until he didn't."

"Do you know where she went?"

"She wrote once from Alibaug." Radhika wiped her hands on her sari, then added, "If she's still there, she'll be by the old ferry jetty. She liked the boats. Said departure was the only honest ceremony left."

Departure.

The word sat heavily.

That evening, Ruhan dug through a flat file in the studio and found a canvas face down, tied with twine. When he cut it free, a half-finished mural emerged—children with kites, a shoreline, storm clouds. In one corner, faint pencil marks read: MV–sky layer, and beneath it, Harish's smaller note: Hold until she returns.

He didn't sleep much after that.

By morning, the decision was made.

Alibaug

The coast smelled of salt, drying nets, motor oil, and monsoon ghosts. Even in the off-season, the ferry jetty held its rhythm—voices, gulls, engines, departures, returns. *The kind of place you could leave forever and still feel as if you'd never left.* Ruhan asked three people before someone recognized the name.

"Madam Meera? The art lady? She teaches kids near the Catholic school now," the fruit-seller told him, slicing guava. "Has white streak in her hair. Laughs in one eye only."

He found her sitting beneath a tarpaulin awning beside a row of painted fishing crates. Children crowded around a long board propped on bricks—painting waves in impossible blues. Meera guided a small boy's hand, steadying his brush without correcting him.

She looked up when she sensed him.

Something flickered in her face. Not recognition—alertness.

"You're not from here," she said.

"No," he admitted.

"You holding something?" she asked, nodding to the envelope in his hand.

He almost laughed. "Yes."

"Then sit. Paint first. Talk after."

He sat cross-legged with the children. She handed him a brush worn flat. He painted a line that was supposed to be a horizon and dissolved into a smear of fading light.

The kids laughed. So did she.

Only after they'd rinsed the buckets and packed the paints did she lower herself onto an upturned crate and say, "Now. The envelope."

He offered it.

She did not open it.

"Who sent you?" she asked.

"My grandfather," Ruhan said. "Harish Desai."

This time the flicker in her eyes was unmistakable.

She leaned back. Closed her eyes for a beat. Then opened the letter.

It took her longer to read those four lines than it had taken him.

When she finished, she refolded it very carefully and held it in both palms like something once warm.

"I thought he chose the canvas over me," she said.

"He wrote that you left before he answered," Ruhan replied.

"I did. I had to." She smiled, not bitterly. "He understood walls. I lived indoors. Neither of us was wrong. Both of us were tired."

"What painting was his?" Ruhan asked. "I found a mural study. Children. Kites."

Meera looked up sharply. "He kept that?"

"He wrote 'Hold until she returns.'"

She laughed once. It broke in the middle.

"I never came back," she said. "But I never stopped writing."

She rose and motioned for him to follow. Behind her small rental cottage sat a metal trunk under a plastic sheet. She dragged it forward, unlatched it, and lifted the lid.

Inside: Letters. Bundled. Unsent.

Some addressed to Harish. Some to Self. Others to Whoever finishes the mural.

Meera looked at him. **"You're carrying his unfinished stories. I've been carrying mine. Let's trade, shall we?"**

Meera sifted through the letters in the trunk like someone searching through fog. Her hands paused over one, not by its label but its worn edge, as if touch had mapped memory onto paper.

"This one," she said. "This one will tell you more than I can."

She didn't offer it to him. She opened it herself.

And read.

Dear Harish,

You once told me you feared forgetting more than loss. That if you forgot how it felt to stand before a wall and see something come alive—a fish, a field, a fist—you would stop being yourself.

I think I feared remembering too much.

You see, there was a morning in Gandhinagar—you probably forgot it—when I came to the studio early. You were hunched over a canvas and didn't hear me come in. I watched you add shadows to a child's face, and it was the gentlest thing I've ever seen.

I wanted to say something. That I felt safe, and seen, and maybe even...beginning to love.

But you looked up, and whatever softness was in you vanished. You smiled that polite smile. You offered chai. You called me "madam" again.

And I knew.

I knew you had folded some piece of you away. I didn't know why. Still don't. Maybe it was shame. Or fear. Or your old ghost of 'shouldn't'.

So, I left.

I wanted to leave like a whisper. No damage. No blame. Just enough silence that you might hear it echo.

You never replied.

Maybe you didn't have the words. Or you thought silence was the reply.

I didn't stop painting. Or writing. Or watching skies shift.

But the mural—the one with the storm above the children? That was us, wasn't it? Joy grounded. Thunder pending.

You should've let it rain.

—M

Silence lingered like perfume. Ruhan looked out at the waterline where boats nodded as if to some unsung rhythm.

"I think," Meera said softly, "your grandfather loved more than he could hold."

"Do you forgive him?"

She folded the letter again. "I forgave him long ago. But I couldn't return. Because what do you return to, when the doorway you left has been bricked up?"

"Maybe you don't return," Ruhan said. "Maybe you start another door. Somewhere else."

She looked at him then, as if seeing not just him, but the thread that had brought him here—the boy tracing shadows to understand the shape of a man now gone.

"Tell me, Ruhan," she said. "Why are you here?"

He thought for a moment. Then answered truthfully.

"Because I'm tired of silence being my inheritance."

That night, she gave him a room with no fan but salt-laced breeze, and in the morning, they walked to the sea. No ceremony. Just paper and paint.

The mural was too fragile to move. But they brought the study—Harish's original canvas—and a new blank panel. They painted side by side. Quietly. The way people do when they have nothing left to prove.

She asked him, once, what his last letter would be if he never wrote another.

He said, "I haven't written it yet."

She didn't press.

On the third day, a boy from the school brought Ruhan a package wrapped in brown paper. Inside were a dozen of Meera's letters—the ones marked To Self—and a note in blue ink:

"These are yours now. Let the studio remember more than just absence."

—M

He packed them carefully.

Before he left, they stood by the mural. The kites had found the wind again. The storm cloud was no longer ominous—just full. Heavy. Ready to rain when needed.

"You know," Meera said, "he never lied in his paintings. Even when he couldn't say what he meant in words."

Ruhan touched the edge of the canvas and nodded.

"He taught me how to leave. I think you're teaching me how to stay."

She smiled, and this time, the laugh didn't break in the middle.

Gandhinagar again.

The studio was not quieter. But it felt more settled when he returned. Like the rooms had inhaled and decided not to exhale until he gave them something.

He unwrapped the mural study and hung it above the drafting desk.

He placed Meera's letters in a small teak box next to the original pile.

And finally—finally—he painted.

It wasn't grand. Or even particularly good.

But it was his. The sea. A lone figure. Two kites. Storm pending.

Below it, he scrawled one line:

"He never answered. But I did."

The old haveli stood quiet, *wrapped in the pale light of late afternoon.* Ruhan stepped down from the veranda and walked with Asha, his mother's old friend, toward a bench beneath a bougainvillaea tree in the courtyard. A few pink petals had drifted onto her shawl. She didn't brush them away.

"I've always believed letters were safer unsent," she said after a while. "Because they can't be misinterpreted if they never leave your hands."

Ruhan studied her profile—time had softened her once sharp features, but there was dignity in her stillness, and grace in her restraint. He understood then what his grandfather must have seen in her.

Asha looked at him suddenly. "Would you like to read what I wrote to Harish?"

He wasn't sure why, but his throat tightened. He nodded.

She disappeared into the house and returned with a small bundle of worn pages tied with golden thread—paper that had yellowed but not crumbled. She placed it in his hands as if offering him something sacred. The pages trembled slightly in the wind.

"I never stopped writing to him," she whispered. "Even after I knew he wouldn't come."

Ruhan untied the thread carefully and read the first letter.

My dearest Harish,

You left like the tide—steady, silent, taking pieces of me that still haven't returned. Do you remember the jasmine you tucked behind my ear the last time we met? I do. It had withered by evening, and yet its scent clung to my pillow for days.

I was angry at first. Then hurt. Then quietly broken. But I never hated you.

Some loves are meant to remain unfinished—not because they weren't real, but because the world wasn't ready for them. We weren't allowed to choose.

But I write these still, for you. For me. For the life we almost lived.

—Asha

Ruhan closed the letter slowly. The edges were soft with time, the ink faded, but the emotion pulsed as if it had just been written. "He never stopped writing either," he murmured. "He just...never sent them."

Asha smiled faintly. "Then maybe we weren't so different after all."

She reached into her shawl and pulled out a second letter, this one newer—written just last week, in what looked like a trembling hand. She handed it to him.

"He came once," she said quietly. "Years ago. He didn't speak much. He only looked around this courtyard, touched the pillar near the steps, and left. I think that was his apology."

Ruhan read the letter aloud:

Asha,

I came to Gandhinagar once, thinking I'd find you. I stood outside your home and heard laughter. Not yours. I didn't knock. I wasn't brave enough.

All these years, I've carried the weight of what we lost. It grew heavier with every Diwali, every monsoon, every jasmine bloom I saw without you.

You deserved more than silence. I hope my letters reached the wind and found your name.

Forgive me. Or don't. But know this: I loved you, always. Even when I didn't dare to say it.

—Harish

Ruhan wiped his eyes before he realized they had welled up. The ache between them was almost reverent—as if sorrow, when shared so honestly, became a kind of devotion.

Asha looked up at the sky, blinking back emotion. "*So many years wasted in silence. So many lives built on fear of speaking one's truth.*"

She turned to him. "Don't let that happen to you, Ruhan. Don't carry letters inside that should have been sent."

He nodded, stunned by the sheer weight of her story and how it echoed his own silence.

"I think," she said gently, "you should write your own letter."

Ruhan hesitated. "To whom?"

She smiled softly. "You'll know."

They sat quietly for a long while. The wind danced through the bougainvillea, and Ruhan's fingers closed around the old letter from Harish, now a bridge between two people who loved and lost without ever truly letting go.

As he walked back through the gate of the haveli, *sunlight brushing his back,* he thought of all the people whose words had never reached their destinations—and how perhaps it wasn't too late to begin sending his own.

Back in his hotel room in Gandhinagar after a few days at the ancestral bungalow, he gazed out of the window as the city lights buzzed faintly beyond. The room was quiet, save for the soft hum of the ceiling fan and the echo of Asha's voice playing on a loop in Ruhan's mind.

Don't carry letters inside that should have been sent.

He sat down at the small desk, pulled out the worn leather notebook he'd kept buried since the day of the funeral, and opened it. Between the pages were two photographs—one of his grandfather standing proud in his army uniform, the other of a younger Harish beside a blooming jasmine tree, smiling in a way Ruhan had never seen in real life.

He gently placed both photos aside, uncapped his pen, and began to write.

To the boy I used to be,

You spent years pretending you didn't need to be heard. You mistook silence for strength and numbness for peace. But now, I see you—hiding behind books, behind sarcasm, behind "I'm fine." I see you trying to be enough for everyone but yourself.

It wasn't your fault that they didn't ask what you were carrying.

But it's your choice now to let go of what they never knew.

This is your letter—not to be mailed or posted—but to be lived. Begin again. Begin truly.

—Ruhan

He exhaled. The release was quiet, but it felt like breathing after holding it in for years. There were still a thousand things left unsaid—to his father, to himself, to the world—but this was a start.

Ruhan slipped the letter into the back pocket of the notebook and closed it with a soft thud. Then, almost instinctively, he picked up the envelope Asha had given him—the last one—and read it again.

Some loves remain unfinished so they can keep us searching. And maybe, in searching, we become whole.

The next morning, he left Gandhinagar early. But before boarding the train, he walked to a small post-box near the station. He stood there for a long while, uncertain.

Then, slowly, he pulled a blank postcard from his bag, scribbled a single line on it, and dropped it in.

It read:

"You were right, Dadu. Some silences are love too."

As the train pulled away from the platform, Ruhan looked out the window—not at the past this time, but at the stretch of unknown ahead.

And for the first time in years, he didn't feel lost.

He felt...ready.

Chapter 11: The Unexpected Past

The day after returning from Gandhinagar, Ruhan found himself strangely unsettled. *There was a quiet, lingering ache in his chest—like someone had plucked a string inside him, and its trembling hadn't ceased.* The conversation with the woman—Lilavati—still echoed in his mind. Her soft voice, her trembling fingers on those old envelopes, her regret-laced smile.

He had felt a shift within him. *Not just about his grandfather. But something else. Something closer.*

That afternoon, the sky was a dull grey, heavy with clouds but not quite raining. Ruhan wandered through the house, restless, as if the walls were growing tighter. Then, almost instinctively, he returned to the attic. The box of letters was still there—though now it felt smaller, lighter. A few letters remained. Maybe four or five.

He sat cross-legged, the wooden floor creaking beneath him. He reached in—and paused.

There was something new. Not a letter. A smaller envelope, tucked under the others, yellowed at the edges. No address. Just a single word on the front:

"Ruhan."

His breath caught.

It wasn't in his grandfather's handwriting.

It was his mother's.

He hadn't seen it in years, but he knew it instantly. The soft curves of her "R", the neat spacing. A strange current ran through his fingers as he opened the envelope. Inside was a folded letter—just one page. The ink had faded, but the words hadn't.

Dear Ruhan,

I don't know if you'll ever read this. Maybe your father will hide it. Maybe the world will. Or maybe you'll find it only when it matters most.

You were only five when I wrote this. Just tall enough to reach the bookshelf and curious enough to rearrange all my poetry books by colour. You never knew how much joy that gave me—your quiet creativity, your strange order in the chaos.

But I fear I won't be around to see you grow into the man I know you'll become. And that fear is heavier than anything I've ever carried.

Your father and I—

We've loved each other once. But now, we are strangers who remember the same house. And your grandfather—he means well. But he is rigid with love. He does not bend, and I—I am too soft to stay unbroken here.

I'm leaving, Ruhan. But not because of you. Never because of you.

I want you to grow up unafraid to love. Unafraid to express. I want you to draw, to paint, to write those letters even if no one reads them. I want you to be everything that this house is afraid of.

If the world ever tells you to harden—don't.

You are allowed to be soft.

Softness is not weakness.

I love you. Always.

—Maa

The attic blurred. Not from dust—but from tears.

He hadn't cried in years. Not like this. Not this ache from a wound he didn't know he had. His mother's face came in flashes. The smell of jasmine. The way she hummed while braiding his hair. The softness she carried like sunlight.

Ruhan sat there for what felt like hours. The letter clutched in one hand, his other resting on the old wooden floor like he was trying to ground himself.

When he finally stood up, the letter still trembling in his grip, he noticed another envelope that had slipped beneath the lining of the box.

Another letter.

Addressed to Anaya.

Anaya?

He didn't recognize the name immediately. But something tugged at his memory. He'd heard it once. Long ago. A whispered conversation, muffled by walls. A nurse? A caretaker?

No.

Another friend of his mother's.

He opened it slowly. His grandfather's handwriting returned.

Dear Anaya,

If this ever reaches you, I want to apologize.

Not for my words—but for my silence.

You tried. You tried to make me understand my son. You tried to explain my daughter-in-law's restlessness. You saw them both clearly, while I saw only shadows of who I wanted them to be. I see now what you meant when you said **"Love is not control. Its presence."**

I thought I was doing the right thing. By being strict. By expecting more. By pushing boundaries.

But in doing so, I drove them apart.

And now, I fear I might lose Ruhan too.

You were right, Anaya.

Love is listening. And I didn't.

Maybe it's too late to fix things.

But I'm writing this in the hope that words might do what I could not.

If Ruhan ever finds this, tell him—

Tell him I tried. In my own way.

Tell him I watched every one of his drawings behind the curtain, even when I pretended I didn't care.

Tell him...I loved him. Fiercely.

And I was just afraid to say it out loud.

—Harish

By the time Ruhan finished reading, it was night. The attic was quiet, but his mind roared.

Two letters.

Two confessions.

Two truths that shattered and rebuilt everything he thought he knew.

Before her death, his mother had walked away for some time—not out of anger, but because the silence in the house had grown too heavy for her to breathe within.

His grandfather had stayed because he didn't know how to break it.

And in the middle stood his father—Ruhan's father—raised between two kinds of silence.

That letter from Harish to his son still sat untouched in the studio.

Ruhan hadn't had the courage to hand it over.

Not yet.

But now...

He saw the layers. The reasons.

He saw the inherited weight they all carried.

Ruhan walked to his room and pinned both letters on the wall above his sketch desk. Then, with trembling fingers, he picked up his pencil and began to draw.

Not a face.

Not a place.

But a moment.

It was the image he carried of his mother—walking away with tears in her eyes, glancing back just once.

A grandfather staring through the curtain at a child sketching dragons.

A boy—somewhere in between—holding two letters in his hand, unsure of which pain to carry first.

When he finished, he titled it quietly.

"The Silence Between Us."

And for the first time in weeks,

Ruhan didn't feel alone.

Morning filtered through the curtains in a soft, warm hush. Ruhan woke early. His fingers still smudged with pencil graphite, his sketch from the night before resting by his desk lamp—hauntingly still.

But something in him had shifted. Not completely healed, but cracked open in a way that sunlight could finally enter.

He sat on the edge of his bed, the two letters—one from his mother, one from his grandfather—now pinned beside his other sketches. They didn't just tell stories. They were the story. Of silence. Of choices. Of love that never learned to speak its own name.

He showered, dressed, and walked down to the kitchen, where his father, as always, was nursing his morning tea, the paper open but unread. The air between them, usually heavy with unsaid things, felt...paused. Still. Like something was waiting to break.

Ruhan sat across from him. Quiet. He reached into his bag and pulled out the another letter he had not read aloud yet.

The the second letter his grandfather had written to his son.

To Ruhan's father.

He placed it on the table.

"Read it," he said. His voice wasn't firm. It wasn't angry. It was...gentle. Like offering a hand.

His father looked at the envelope. Then at Ruhan. A beat of recognition crossed his eyes—he knew the handwriting. Slowly, without a word, he unfolded the letter.

The silence in the kitchen was not tense this time. It was reverent. When he finished reading, his hands trembled just slightly. The paper remained in his grip longer than necessary. His face was unreadable, but his eyes—his eyes were soft.

He looked at Ruhan, blinking.

"I didn't know," he said, finally. "He never told me any of this."

Ruhan gave a small nod. "He didn't tell me either. But he told the paper."

His father gave a bitter half-chuckle. "Maybe we're a family of men who only talk to paper."

Ruhan smiled—wry, but real.

There was a long pause, then something surprising. His father whispered, "**She would have wanted you to know her, Ruhan.**"

It took Ruhan a moment to register who she meant. His mother.

"She left," Ruhan said.

"She had to," his father replied. "You were too young. I never spoke of her because I thought...shielding you was the right thing. But I think...I was shielding myself."

The honesty hurt. But it was also the first real thing Ruhan had heard from his father in years.

"I wish she had stayed," Ruhan said quietly.

"I wish I had asked her to," his father whispered back.

Their words didn't fix the past. But they didn't fall into silence either.

And that was something.

Later that afternoon, Ruhan went to the town library—an old building with crooked bookshelves and dusty corners. The librarian, a quiet woman with thick glasses and a smile like faded paper, greeted him with a nod.

He asked for records. Photos. Archives.

He wanted to know more about his mother. Not the version his grandfather feared. Not the silence his father buried. But her.

He found a photo in an old art competition archive. She stood beside a canvas, vibrant and alive, her curls loosely tied, her eyes bright. The title below her name read:

"To Be Soft in a World That Breaks You."

A tear rolled down Ruhan's cheek.

God, he thought, I'm her son.

As he walked out of the library, a memory returned. He was maybe five or six. He had been scared one night of a thunderstorm. And she had told him,

"Listen, baby. ***Thunder is just the sky's way of saying it feels too much.*** *And feeling too much is okay.*"

He stopped walking. Looked up.

It was about to rain.

And for once, he wasn't afraid.

That evening, before going back home, he returned to the attic one last time. Not for the letters. But for the box itself.

He emptied it. Folded the edges. Took it downstairs and placed it in the garden. There, he lit it on fire.

The flames caught quickly.

Old paper curling.

Ash rising like a memory.

It wasn't an erasure.

It was a ritual.

A farewell.

To everything that went unsaid.

And a beginning.

To everything that still could be.

That night, Ruhan began writing again. But not to strangers.

Not to the ghosts.

He began writing to himself.

Chapter 12: The Rival

The day had barely stirred. Gandhinagar lingered in the mist of dawn, its silence carried with him as he returned to his father's house—no longer empty, but listening.

He sat cross-legged on the floor, the morning light cutting slanted paths across the wooden planks. The box of letters, frayed and reluctant, lay beside him once again. His hands moved almost instinctively now, trained by nights of quiet excavation. Paper had become a language of its own, and Ruhan its reader—deciphering the voices of ghosts.

He was no longer searching for anything in particular; the story had begun to write itself. And then he found it.

A thin envelope, older than the rest. The ink was nearly faded, the paper brittle at the edges. There was no name on the outside, just a single word in his grandfather's sharp, unwavering script:

"Rival."

Ruhan hesitated. The word felt...foreign. All the other letters had been named—to sons, lovers, soldiers, strangers. This was different. Impersonal, almost. He turned it over, fingers brushing the seal, and broke it open.

"To the man who shadowed my every step—

And made me question mine..."

The first line pulled the breath from his lungs. There was something deeply unsaid in those few words—a wound, perhaps. A debt. *A mirror.*

He unfolded the letter carefully, its weight more than paper alone.

Harish's Letter (excerpt):

You were not just my competitor. You were my constant reminder. That I was never the best—only first. You came after, but you did everything better. Sharper, faster, cleaner. And while the world called it fair play, I often let envy call it theft.

I've held your name between my teeth like iron for years, tasting blood, never spitting it out. I feared what it would mean to admit: I respected you. Even when I wished you would fail.

You built what I couldn't. You understood people in a way I never did. And yet, I always felt I had to win—not for success, but to prove I mattered more.

But here's the truth: ***You were never my enemy. My ego was.***

If this letter reaches your hands, I ask nothing. Only that you know: I carried your shadow as if it were my own.

Ruhan sat still.

This was the first time he'd seen his grandfather bend without breaking. All the other letters bore weight—of silence, of sorrow, of love unspoken—but this one...this one carried surrender.

He folded the letter slowly, reverently.

There was an address scribbled faintly on the back—a name, too, though part of it had been smudged by time.

"Shyamlal Mehta—Mehta Tools & Fabrication, Ranip Industrial Zone."

He looked it up. It still existed. A small manufacturing unit. Old-school. Family-run.

There was no question now.

He'd go meet the man his grandfather once saw as his reflection—his flaw.

And maybe, in that confrontation, Ruhan would come face-to-face with a version of himself, too.

The Ranip Industrial Zone was nothing like the postcard edges of Gandhinagar. It breathed metal and dust, a worn-out rhythm of machines groaning to life and tired men who moved with purpose. As Ruhan stepped out of the auto, the sun had already begun to press down against the aluminum rooftops, casting distorted reflections over the oil-stained pavements.

The address led him to a narrow gate with faded blue paint that read:

Mehta Tools & Fabrication

The bell above the gate clanged as he pushed it open. Inside the workshop, rows of steel beams and grinding sparks danced behind wire mesh. Men in grey uniforms worked with focused urgency, and above it all, a small glass cabin overlooked the floor like a crow's nest.

"Who are you looking for?" asked a lean man in his forties, wiping his hands on a rag.

"I'm here to meet Mr. Shyamlal Mehta," Ruhan replied, steadying his voice. "I...have a letter that belonged to him."

The man's expression shifted just slightly, as if an old memory stirred behind his eyes. "He's upstairs. Office cabin. You'll need to wait a minute."

Ruhan nodded, suddenly aware of the thudding in his chest. This wasn't like meeting the woman from the first letter, or listening to a veteran's silence. This felt closer to looking into a cracked mirror—not to mourn, but to understand.

Within minutes, the cabin door creaked open. An elderly man emerged, tall and surprisingly well-kept for his age. His hair was silver but combed immaculately back, and his eyes had the alertness of someone who had never truly retired.

"You're Harish's grandson," he said. Not a question. A fact.

Ruhan blinked, startled. "Yes. How did you...?"

"I'd know those eyes anywhere," Shyamlal said with a faint smile. "They used to watch me like hawks across boardrooms and tenders."

He motioned for Ruhan to come in.

The office smelled of old paper and soldering fumes. On the wall hung faded newspaper clippings—one of which bore the names Harish Engineering and Mehta Tools in bold, dated typeface: "A Battle for the Bypass Bridge Contract."

"I read his letter," Ruhan said once they sat down. "He... never sent it."

Shyamlal leaned back, folding his hands over his chest. "He wouldn't have. That wasn't his way. *Harish wore pride like armour.*"

Ruhan handed him the folded sheet. Shyamlal took it in silence, reading each line slowly—without tears, but not without weight. When he finished, he didn't speak right away.

Finally, he said, "Your grandfather was the most stubborn man I've ever met. We were both young, both desperate to leave our mark. And we did—sometimes by stepping on each other's dreams."

Ruhan tilted his head. "Did you hate him?"

Shyamlal chuckled, the sound dry and bitter. "No. I envied him. He had conviction, even when he was wrong. I doubted myself every step of the way. He...never let the world see that crack."

"But he did crack," Ruhan whispered, almost to himself.

Shyamlal looked at him, a silence hanging like a held breath. "Yes. I saw it once. At the bridge site. We were losing a contract we both wanted—to someone neither of us could stand. I remember him standing there, looking out over the cement pillars rising from the Sabarmati, and he said, 'Maybe none of this matters if we both forget why we began.'"

Ruhan's voice caught in his throat. "He never told anyone that."

"He wouldn't," Shyamlal said. "Admitting doubt wasn't in his vocabulary. But I think...I think that was the moment we stopped being rivals. And just became two old men trying to matter."

Ruhan sat quietly for a moment, the hum of the factory outside fading into something softer, almost meditative.

"I used to think legacy meant being remembered," he said finally. "Now I wonder if it's just about making peace—with ourselves and with those we couldn't forgive."

Shyamlal looked at him with something close to tenderness. "Your grandfather never apologized to me, not really. But this letter? This is more than enough."

They stood together, not as extensions of old wounds, but as men who had inherited scars—and the choice of what to do with them.

As Ruhan left, Shyamlal called out, "You look more like him than you know. But the difference? *You came back.*"

The ride back to his guesthouse was quiet—unnaturally so. Gandhinagar's rhythm passed by Ruhan in blurs of green, stone, and steel. But inside his mind, things were louder: his grandfather's voice, the unsent words, the bridges never crossed.

And now—a man once seen as a rival, offering not bitterness, but peace.

In the quiet of the evening, Ruhan sat by the small writing desk near the window, Shyamlal's words echoing in the corners of his thoughts.

You came back.

It sounded simple. But it wasn't.

Coming back—to a story you never knew you were a part of, to wounds you never made but inherited, to fears shaped by absence—was never simple.

He placed the letter down again. The folds had grown softer now, edges a little frayed by repeated openings—like the truth, growing gentler the more it's seen.

For years, he had been afraid of becoming a shadow—someone who lived behind other people's stories: his father's bitterness, his grandfather's silences, even the unspoken expectations of being someone that he would never measure up to, that he would never create something worthy on his own.

But today shifted something.

Shyamlal's admission hadn't just added depth to Harish's past. It had shown Ruhan something else—that legacies weren't built only in triumphs. Sometimes, they were built in regret. In unsaid words. In gestures that came decades late, but still mattered.

He thought back to the bridge they had once fought over—imagined both men standing there, equally exhausted, equally desperate. He wondered if Harish ever returned to it again in his mind. Wondered if that was the day he began to collect the letters he never sent.

Ruhan took out his journal, the one he'd barely touched since this journey began. Pages blank, ink untouched. But now, for the first time in weeks, he began to write.

Legacy isn't what we leave behind in stone and steel.

It's the ache we carry to be understood—even when it's too late.

And sometimes, the loudest truths are hidden in the things we couldn't say out loud.

I've been running from the fear that I'll never be enough.

But maybe it's not about being more than them.

Maybe it's about being fully myself—with all the mess, all the softness, all the questions.

And maybe that's enough.

He closed the journal softly, tears not of grief but of release filling his eyes.

The letters had once felt like ghosts of a man he barely knew. Now they felt like doors.

And with every one he read—and every truth he uncovered—*another room lit up in the darkened house of his past.*

That night, Ruhan stood on the rooftop under the vast Gandhinagar sky. The air was warm, the stars faint through the city's glow. Yet something about the silence felt different. Not empty—but full.

He wasn't done.

There were more letters to find. More lives to meet. More truths buried in the ink of a grandfather who couldn't speak what he felt—but had written it down for someone, someday, to read.

And Ruhan, finally, was ready to listen.

ACT III: Closure & Clarity

"Healing isn't rewriting the past.

It's choosing to carry it differently—with open hands instead of closed fists."

Chapter 13: Reaching the Artist Within

It began with charcoal smudges and silence.

Ruhan sat in the attic, knees drawn up, his sketchbook trembling in his lap. The sunlight broke through the wooden slats above, pouring dust-motes over his fingers like whispered blessings. Around him, the letters lay in careful disorder—some folded, some open, others reread so many times their creases had turned soft.

Each letter carried a face now. A name. A heartbeat.

They were no longer just words left behind—they were echoes of lives interrupted.

And he...

He had carried them inside his chest for too long.

The need to do something with them grew unbearable.

Ruhan turned to the blank wall of the studio. Once bare, once untouched—a wall that had stood as still and silent as he had felt all these years. *Now it called to him like a memory waiting to be painted.*

He picked up the first brush.

The first strokes were hesitant—like writing in a language he had once known but forgotten. *He didn't try to paint faces at first. He let the emotions lead: a swirl of ash-grey for sorrow, blood-rust for the bitterness, ochre for the forgotten warmth.*

Then came the eyes.

A child's eyes, wide with loss.

A woman's eyes, tired yet tender.

An old soldier's eyes, sharp as cracked glass.

Each pair emerged from his brush as if summoned—*not imagined but remembered. As if Ruhan had known them his whole life.*

He worked in silence for hours, sometimes days, barely eating, barely sleeping. The wall became a map of souls—layered, interwoven. He didn't care about technique. His lines were raw, bold, broken. His colours bled into one another. Faces overlapped, like memories fighting for space.

He called it Voices Never Heard.

It wasn't just art.

It was a confession.

Every letter had whispered something into him—an unfinished story, a breath never exhaled. And now, he was giving it form. He painted Lilavati's hands holding a flower that had long withered. Himmat Singh's silhouette standing alone on a battlefield of shadows. The stranger's quiet gaze lingering like a question. Even the rival—his bitterness melting into something more human than hate.

And then—

His grandfather's eyes.

He painted them last. Not the version frozen in the funeral photograph. But younger. Softer. Filled with guilt, yes, but also love.

In painting them, Ruhan realized something he hadn't understood until now:

Harish hadn't been perfect. He had loved, failed, hurt, forgiven—and still couldn't say the words he should've.

But maybe that was the point.

Maybe love wasn't perfect. Maybe it wasn't loud.

Maybe it was letters never sent, walls never painted, eyes that carried both truth and fear.

And now, through him—through this mural—it could be released.

As he stepped back to view the completed mural, a strange hush fell around him. *Not silence—no, not that—but a sacred stillness, like the kind inside temples where memories kneel beside prayers.*

The room had changed.

Or perhaps he had.

Each figure on the wall looked back at him, as if waiting. Not for approval. But for acknowledgment.

For being seen.

Ruhan wiped his paint-streaked hands on an old rag. His fingers trembled—not from exhaustion, but from something deeper. The kind of trembling that follows catharsis.

He sat cross-legged on the studio floor, the smell of paint thick in the air, sunlight slicing across the mural in golden angles.

He thought about the title again: Voices Never Heard.

But now, they had been.

Through his brush, through his body, through every crack he had carried—they had spoken. And he had listened.

He pulled out the box once more—the letters, the lives, the legacy—and held them close.

For the first time, he didn't feel like just a carrier of grief.

He felt like a storyteller.

An artist.

A bridge.

His own voice, once buried beneath silence, was rising—*not in volume, but in clarity.*

This wasn't the end.

There were still letters to deliver.

Words to say.

Truths to meet.

And one letter—unfinished, untouched—still waited for him at the bottom of the box. Addressed not to the past...

...but to the present.

To his father.

Ruhan looked up at the mural one last time before turning toward the studio table. He picked up a fresh sheet of paper. The ink took its time flowing.

But this time, he was ready to write.

Chapter 14: The Final Letter

The flat was quiet. Too quiet.

It wasn't the gentle kind of silence that invites peace—this was the kind that presses inwards, echoing thoughts against the ribs. The kitchen window rattled faintly with the evening breeze, but Ruhan didn't notice. His eyes remained fixed on the envelope in his hand.

He had found it tucked between the pages of a hardcover diary—the same one where Harish kept records of yearly taxes and repair receipts. *Almost like he'd hidden this one where no one would go looking for emotion.*

The envelope simply read:

"To My Son."

The absence of embellishment made it heavier.

Not Dear son, not My beloved, not even a date.

Just the flat, unsoftened truth.

A long breath rose in Ruhan's chest, but he didn't find the courage to let it go. He stared at the letter for nearly twenty minutes, sitting alone on the living room floor, surrounded by the weight of everything the past few weeks had brought. Letters. Secrets. Shadows. Truths that didn't just belong to others anymore, but were now shaping him.

This letter wasn't about someone else.

It was about them.

It was his family's final reckoning.

And perhaps, it was time.

It was late when Ruhan finally called.

A single ring, then a pause. Then again. A part of him hoped his father wouldn't pick up.

He did.

"Hello?" came the voice. Familiar, low, worn.

"Baba," Ruhan said softly. "Can you...come here tomorrow morning? I found something. You should see it."

A pause.

"I'll come," his father said and hung up.

Morning

Ruhan had never made tea this carefully in his life. The kettle sang long before he remembered to pour it. He kept adjusting the two cups on the table—unsure if his father would even want one. Unsure of everything, really.

When the doorbell rang, his breath caught.

He opened the door to find his father standing in that same white half-sleeved shirt he always wore for "serious things." He looked slightly out of place in Ruhan's studio flat—no old wall clocks, no framed gods, no loud TV humming in the background. Just sunlight and silence.

Ruhan gestured him in.

His father removed his sandals without being asked. He noticed the small cactus on the windowsill, the folded blankets, the scattered sketchbooks—all the things Ruhan thought he'd never see.

"You live quietly," he said, finally.

"I try," Ruhan replied.

They stood in silence again. Then Ruhan walked to the dining table and picked up the envelope.

"I didn't open it," he said. "I thought...you should."

He extended it toward his father like one would offer a flame.

The old man didn't reach for it immediately. He stared at it, lips pressed together, a storm quietly rising behind his eyes.

"What is this?" he asked, though something in his voice said he already knew.

Ruhan's throat tightened. **"The final one. From Dadu."**

A flicker passed through his father's expression—disbelief, anger, regret, all tangled into one. But he took the envelope.

He sat down.

Ruhan watched his hands shake slightly as he unfolded the letter.

And then, silence.

His eyes moved slowly over the words.

Lines. Paragraphs. Regrets inked decades too late.

He read the letter once. Then again.

And then, as if air had been knocked out of him, he whispered,

"He wrote this for me."

His voice cracked on the last word.

My son,

You were always a mirror I couldn't face. A softness I mistook for weakness, a light I convinced myself would burn out if not hardened. I taught you silence, thinking it would make you strong. But it only made you lonely.

And for that, I carry shame beyond what I can say.

I remember your first drawing—a dragon with crooked wings and too many teeth. You showed it to me with eyes full of wonder. And I said nothing. I thought silence was discipline. I didn't realise it was a wound.

You grew up thinking my silence meant disappointment.

It didn't. It meant I didn't know how to be a father.

You didn't fail me. I failed you.

And though I cannot undo the years, I can leave this truth behind:

You were never the problem.

I was just too broken to love you loudly.

Forgive me, if you can. And if not, just...know this: I loved you. Even when I couldn't show it.

Your father,

Harish

By the time the letter was folded again, Ruhan's father was no longer sitting upright. His head hung low, shoulders shaking in a way Ruhan had never seen before.

He wept. Quietly, but fully.

Decades of silence, finally unwrapped.

"I waited my whole life..." he whispered, voice crumbling, "for him to say something like this."

Ruhan sat down beside him, unsure if he should touch him, unsure if this moment needed words or just presence.

"I hated him," his father continued. "Not for what he did. But for what he didn't do. For what he never said. And now..." He looked at the letter again. "Now he says it when he's gone."

"He said it," Ruhan replied. "That matters."

His father nodded, but then looked at him—really looked. **"I became like him, didn't I?"**

"You tried not to," Ruhan said. "But...yeah. A little."

There was no anger in his voice. Only truth.

And truth, for once, didn't shatter anything.

It softened.

"I didn't know how to be different," his father said. "No one teaches you. You just copy what you saw."

"You can stop copying now," Ruhan said.

They both looked at each other.

And then his father did something he hadn't done in years—he reached out. Not a formal, stiff handshake. But a slow, trembling hand on his son's shoulder.

"I'm sorry, Ruhan."

Ruhan closed his eyes. Let the weight of it settle.

It was too late for Harish and his son.

But maybe not too late for the next father and son.

That night, when his father had gone, Ruhan walked out to his balcony and looked at the sky. The stars were clear. The air still.

He opened his sketchbook. For the first time in days, he didn't feel hollow.

He didn't feel like he was holding someone else's pain anymore.

He felt like he understood his own.

And then, he did something he never expected.

He wrote a letter.

Not to the past.

Not even to his father.

But to himself.

To the boy who kept drawing dragons,

You were never too sensitive. Never too soft. You were light in a dark place.

And now, you've become fire.

—Ruhan.

The studio was quieter now. But not empty.

The kind of quiet that follows a storm—when leaves still tremble, when soil still breathes from the weight of rain. Harish's letter rested on the table, between a half-drunk cup of chai and a napkin Ruhan had wordlessly offered his father when he broke down.

They hadn't spoken much since. The air between them felt like a fresh wound—too raw to press, too important to ignore.

His father cleared his throat.

"You remember that art competition in your school?" he asked suddenly. "You were, what, nine?"

Ruhan looked up, surprised. "The one where I came third?"

"You made a painting of a bird flying from a cage. I remember."

He smiled faintly. "I kept the painting. It's still in the old cupboard, behind your report cards."

Ruhan blinked.

All these years...he had thought that painting was discarded. Forgotten. Like most of his childhood efforts. That faint smile on his father's face—it was the first time he realized that his silence hadn't been emptiness. *It had been... an inability.*

"You never said anything."

"I didn't know how. I thought pride had to be...loud. A trophy, a medal. But I was proud. Every time."

Ruhan swallowed. A soft ache blossomed in his chest.

"I used to imagine you hated my art," he said.

His father's face broke.

"I didn't. I was just afraid you'd fail. I thought if I didn't praise it, you'd grow stronger. Learn to survive rejection."

"But rejection came anyway," Ruhan said, voice low. "It came...from you."

The words didn't land like blame. *They landed like truth—painful, but necessary.*

His father nodded slowly.

"I know," he whispered. "And I regret that more than anything."

They both stared at the letter again. The final confession of a man who couldn't speak until death took away the choice. *Maybe that was Harish's way of loving—quiet, flawed, unseen.* But he had loved. And he had written.

It was something.

They talked for hours that morning. About little things. About the big things.

His father asked questions he'd never asked before.

"Do you still draw dragons?"

"Do you ever miss your mother?"

"Why didn't you come home for Diwali that year?"

And Ruhan answered them.

Not because he wanted to reopen old wounds, but because he finally felt safe enough not to lie.

There was a strange kind of closeness building in the spaces between their words—fragile, tentative, but very, very real. Like two broken people, realising they could still build something from the pieces.

That evening, after his father left, Ruhan found himself staring at the letter again.

This time, he copied it into his journal—word for word—in his own handwriting.

It felt necessary. *Like tracing the lines of a scar so it wouldn't disappear.* Like acknowledging what had shaped him.

Then he did something even more unusual.

He took a blank page and wrote back.

Dear Dadu,

I wish you had said this while you were alive. I wish Baba had heard your voice instead of ink. I wish I didn't have to grow up in the silence you left behind.

But still—thank you.

For finally saying it.

For trying.

This letter...it changed something. Not just in him. But in me.

We're talking now.

And maybe...one day, we'll be okay.

I hope wherever you are, you know that I don't hate you.

I truly wish we all knew better.

—Ruhan

He folded it and tucked it into the envelope with Harish's letter—sealing both together.

Unsent words, finally finding rest.

A Week Later

Ruhan visited home.

Not for any occasion. No funeral. No obligation. Just...a visit.

He stepped into the courtyard he had once called a cage.

The neem tree still stood tall. The swing still creaked faintly in the wind. But something was different. *The house no longer felt like a graveyard of things unsaid. It felt like a place that could breathe again.*

His father greeted him with chai and awkward warmth. But this time, Ruhan didn't shrink from it. He sat beside him on the charpai and looked around.

"Dadu's coat," he said suddenly, spotting it hanging behind the door.

His father followed his gaze.

"He always kept it pressed, even when he had nowhere to go."

Ruhan smiled faintly. "I want to keep it."

His father hesitated for a moment, then nodded. "It's yours."

The coat felt heavy when Ruhan took it in his hands—not just in fabric, but in memory. He ran his fingers across the buttons, the torn lining, the scent of mothballs and old winter days.

"Do you ever miss him?" he asked.

His father looked away. **"I miss what could've been."**

Ruhan understood.

That night, before returning to Gandhinagar, Ruhan visited the old storage box one last time. He pulled out some letters to keep—not all of them. Just a few.

One from Himmat Singh.

One from Lilavati.

One from the stranger in the railway café.

And, of course, Harish's final letter.

He placed them into a leather folder and sealed it.

This wasn't just a collection of other people's stories anymore.

It was his legacy now.

Before the Chapter Ends

Ruhan sat in his train seat, sketchbook open on his lap, the countryside blurring past the window.

He didn't feel like he was running anymore.

He didn't feel like a ghost in his own story.

He felt...ready.

Ready to create again.

Ready to write.

Ready to live.

And maybe—just maybe—ready to forgive.

As the sun dipped behind the fields, Ruhan turned to the first blank page and wrote:

"This story began with a funeral.

But it ends with a return."

Chapter 15: To Whom It Never Reached

The sky over Gandhinagar had turned a moody grey, as if it, too, sensed the quiet tremor in Ruhan's chest.

The studio smelled faintly of turpentine and drying paint, his mural "Voices Never Heard" still dominating the far wall—bold strokes of emotion and memory sealed into form. Every story he had touched, every letter he had read, lived here now. But something still buzzed under the surface of his skin, *like a sentence not yet said.*

That morning, he hadn't planned to return to the attic.

But something had tugged at him, and there he stood again—amidst the dust and cobwebs of stories past—brushing his fingers along the familiar rusted box. He had opened it a dozen times before. He knew every edge, every fold, every scent. Or so he believed.

Until he lifted the base.

There, pressed between the wood and the bottom of the box, was a hidden slit. And in it—a single, unfinished letter.

The envelope bore no date.

Just one name in fading blue ink:

Ruhan.

His name. Not his father's. Not some stranger's. His.

His fingers shook as he slid the fragile paper out. The handwriting was unmistakably his grandfather's—strong in its strokes but hesitant at the edges, *as if each word had been earned through struggle.*

He began to read.

"Dear Ruhan,"

"I don't know if this letter will ever find you. Perhaps I'm too late, or perhaps I never found the courage to give it. But I need to say this anyway."

"I have watched you from a distance—not just in miles, but in silence. You remind me of the man I once wanted to be. Not the one I became."

"You are gentler than I allowed myself to be. And for that, I am both proud and ashamed."

"I never knew how to tell you I loved you."

That was it.

The ink stopped mid-sentence. No period. No sign-off. No neat closure.

Just...silence.

Ruhan stared at the last word, his throat tightening.

Loved.

Did he?

Or, had he simply wished, all along, that he had known better?

The attic suddenly felt too small, too loud in its quiet. His chest ached with questions he had buried beneath sarcasm, distance, and years of trying not to care. But the truth was—he had cared.

He always had.

Ruhan sat in the corner of the studio floor that night, the letter in his lap and the lamp casting gold across the paint-splattered tiles.

His mind spiralled through memories—every moment of approval he had craved, every awkward hug he had hoped for, every silence he had mistaken for anger when *it was just fear. Fear of failure. Fear of connection. Fear of love.*

Maybe his grandfather hadn't known how to speak.

Maybe that's why he wrote.

But Ruhan wasn't sure anymore if even writing was enough.

The words in the letter burned holes into him—not because they were harsh, but because they weren't finished.

He ran his hands through his hair and whispered, "**What am I supposed to do with half a goodbye?**"

Then it came to him, like breath drawn after a long underwater silence.

He had to answer.

No—he had to finish it.

The sun had just begun to slip into the folds of the horizon when Ruhan sat alone in the studio once more—the walls dappled with the golden breath of evening light. "Voices Never Heard" stood complete on the far wall, yet the silence it had once embodied still hummed in the air like an unfinished chord.

A letter lay before him—the final, unsent one—not from his grandfather, but from himself.

The past had spoken.

Now, it was his turn.

He pulled the chair closer, the legs scraping against the floor like a violin bow over worn strings. His fingers brushed against the edges of the paper, and for a brief moment, he hesitated. *What do you write when you are writing to the ache inside yourself?* To the generations before you? To everything that was never spoken?

He picked up the pen and began.

To Whom It Never Reached,

I've spent nights listening to the quiet you left behind. Reading your words. Painting your grief. Walking through your memories like they were mine. I thought I came here to understand you. ***But somewhere along the way, I found me.***

Your silence taught me to speak. Your pain taught me to feel. Your regret—it taught me how to forgive, and how to stop holding my breath when I say the word "love."

You never sent these letters because maybe you thought it wouldn't matter. Or you feared they wouldn't be heard. But they mattered to me. Every forgotten sentence. Every ink-stained fold. Every word scratched out. I listened. I stayed. And now, it's my turn.

So, this is my letter—not just to you, but to everything I never said either.

To my father, I forgive you, not because you asked, but because I deserve to move on.

To my younger self, I'm sorry for doubting your softness. It was your greatest strength.

To the quiet, the broken, the lost—your voice matters, even if no one answers.

And to you, Dadu—thank you for the letters. Thank you for not sending them. Thank you for letting me find them when I needed them most.

You never reached the ones you wrote to.

But you reached me.

And now, I will reach others.

—Ruhan

The paper trembled slightly as he folded it, but his hands did not. The weight of grief had been shared. The cycle was broken. He placed the letter into an envelope—no name, no address. Just one sentence scrawled on the front: To Whom It Never Reached.

He didn't post it.

He framed it.

And hung it beside the mural.

Months Later

The studio had transformed. Not into a gallery—but into a sanctuary.

At the entrance hung a sign, hand-painted and slightly crooked:

"To Whom It Never Reached—An Exhibition of Unsent Letters, Unspoken Truths, and Unfinished Stories"

Visitors arrived with hearts like unopened boxes. Some came with nothing but curiosity. Others came carrying years. Ruhan welcomed none of them with speeches. Instead, he let the art speak. Let the walls whisper.

The mural—Voices Never Heard—stood at the heart of the room. Around it bloomed letters pinned by visitors. Folded notes. Postcards. Scribbled napkins. Some were poetic. Some were raw. *Some were just dates, names, and a tearstain.*

A child pinned a drawing of her lost dog.

A young woman left a letter to the version of herself she never got to be.

An old man slipped in quietly, read the letter framed on the wall, and left a single white feather below it.

And Ruhan?

He sat in the corner with a worn-out journal on his lap. *Sketching. Smiling. Watching healing take form in ink, paper, and silence.*

A woman approached him once—eyes brimming with the kind of ache that had no name.

"Is it okay," she asked softly, "if my letter is just...empty?"

He nodded. ***"Even silence deserves a place."***

That night, when the lights dimmed and the visitors left, Ruhan stood in front of the mural alone.

And for the first time in months, he didn't feel alone at all.

He touched the corner where a boy had once stood with a letter in his hand and painted one last detail—a single open envelope, with wings.

Then stepped back.

Smiled.

And whispered,

"At last, silence had found its voice."

Epilogue: The Gallery of Unspoken Things

Six Months Later—Ahmedabad, Gujarat

The gallery stood quietly on a narrow street, *tucked between a forgotten bookstore and a café that smelled of cinnamon and old dreams.* A soft signboard read:

"To Whom It Never Reached"

An Exhibition of Letters, Memories, and Silent Voice

Curated by Ruhan Desai

Inside, the walls were not white, but textured—*raw like unfinished thoughts.* There was no formal lighting; rather, warm amber hues casting gentle shadows. And on those walls lived Ruhan's soul.

Each corner held a piece of someone else's silence:

A torn envelope.

A faded photograph.

A yellowed letter folded so many times it had nearly dissolved.

And then there was the mural.

The massive, breathing mural.

"Voices Never Heard."

Faces—old and young, Indian and foreign, some smiling, some unfinished—emerged from brushstrokes that danced and collided. Each figure whispered something. Grief. Love. Regret. Hope. *It wasn't loud. But it lingered.*

Beneath the mural, a wooden box stood—carved with words that once meant everything to him:

"Write the letter you never sent."

People did.

Strangers. Couples. Survivors. Sons. Mothers.

They scribbled letters on recycled paper, some trembling, some defiant, and slipped them into the box with no return address.

No names. Just weight.

Ruhan watched from a corner—not as a host, but as a participant.

His father stood beside him, not touching, but present.

Still awkward. Still stitched with quiet. But there.

"A lot of people showed up," his father said, eyes on the box.

"A lot of people had something to say," Ruhan replied.

A pause.

"I read your letter," his father murmured. "Still don't know how to reply."

"**You just did,**" Ruhan said quietly.

And in that moment—it was enough.

As the sun dipped, casting a golden haze over the letters and faces, Ruhan took one last folded paper from his pocket. The unfinished letter from his grandfather—the one meant for him.

He placed it gently under the mural.

Not to display.

Not to explain.

But to complete.

And then he walked out into the open air, the sound of healing trailing behind him like the scent of rain on dust.

Closing Note

To the ones who stayed silent.

To the voices tucked away in drawers, never mailed.

To the heartbreak that never found the right words,

and the apologies written too late—

This story was for you.

If there's a letter still sitting inside you,

half-formed, unsent, afraid to reach—

may you find the courage

to write it anyway.

Because healing doesn't always come

with answers.

Sometimes,

it begins with the act of finally speaking.

—Bhavya Barai

To Whom It Never Reached

Acknowledgments

This book began as a whisper and grew into a voice—not just mine, but of every silence I've ever carried.

To the **storytellers**—those *who speak in fragments, in memories, in brushstrokes and broken sentences*: thank you for reminding me that stories don't always need to be loud to be heard.

To the **strangers**—the ones who left feathers, folded notes, or just a glance across the room: *you may not know it, but you live in these pages.*

To my family, for loving me in the moments I could not love myself, and for teaching me that even silence holds meaning.

To every soul who shared their stories with me—through letters, glances, or lingering pauses—*you unknowingly wrote parts of this book.*

To my readers, especially those who found pieces of themselves in these pages: *thank you for carrying this journey forward.* Your presence gives the unwritten words a place to land.

To my inner child—*the dreamer with trembling hands and a stubborn heart—you never gave up. This is yours.*

And lastly, to the letters that never reached—may this be the place where they finally do.

About the Author

Bhavya Barai is a 22-year-old engineer by degree and a storyteller by soul—a quiet force from Gujarat who doesn't just write stories but *gathers* them. A recipient of the ***21st Century Emily Dickinson Award***, he began his literary journey with *Whispers from Earth and Soul*, a poetic debut that gave voice to the silences we carry.

In his second book, To Whom It Never Reached, he dives deeper into themes of memory, heritage, and healing—exploring *the ache of unsent letters and the weight of things left unsaid.* Bhavya collects the world in fragments: *river-washed stones, forgotten feathers, old keychains, and origami dinosaurs gifted to strangers on trains*—each one transformed into ink on the page.

While currently pursuing further studies in a field closely tied to his engineering background, his heart continues to belong to words. When not writing, he's often found cooking like an artist with spices, sketching ideas yet to be built, or wandering with a pen behind his ear and pockets full of quiet treasures—*always chasing stories even the wind forgets.*

He shares intimate fragments of this evolving universe on Instagram: @bhavya.barai_